Praise for Vicki

"It's a wonderful sexy r[...]
appealing and likable c[...]
going to delve into mor[...]
Brotherhood series."
—*HarlequinJunkie*, Top Pick, on *Cowboy Untamed*

"The tongue-in-cheek, sweet yet sensual and
comfortable family feel...remains until the last page.
Cowboy After Dark is a story that will keep you
smiling."
—*RT Book Reviews*, Top Pick, on *Cowboy After Dark*

"Thompson continues to do what she does best,
tying together strong family values bound by blood
and choice, interspersed with the more sizzling
aspects of the relationship."
—*RT Book Reviews* on *Thunderstruck*

"All the characters, background stories and
character development are positively stellar;
the warm family feeling is not saccharine-sweet,
but heartfelt and genuine, and Lexi and Cade's
rekindled romance is believable from beginning to
end, along with the classy, sexy and tender love
scenes."
—*Fresh Fiction* on *Midnight Thunder*

"Vicki Lewis Thompson has compiled a tale of
this terrific family, along with their friends and
employees, to keep you glued to the page and
ending with that warm and loving feeling."
—*Fresh Fiction* on *Cowboys and Angels*

Dear Reader,

Welcome to Thunder Mountain Ranch! Many of you have been with me since Cade Gallagher drove in at dawn with a horse in the trailer and a cat named Ringo on the front seat of his pickup. I thank you for spending so much time with the family! We've had some good times together. Matt Forrest's story kicks off another summer of yummy cowboys who are proud to be part of the Harlequin Special Edition lineup. Yee-haw!

For those of you who are just discovering the world of the Thunder Mountain Brotherhood, go ahead and dive right in! I promise you won't get lost. I can't wait for you to fall in love with Rosie and Herb, the foster parents who turned their ranch into a haven for homeless boys many years ago. The boys grew into men who all abide by the cowboy code of honor, and the ranch has become an equine education facility for teens. Sound like fun?

Trust me, it will be, especially when Matt comes home! This cowboy turned movie star landed a starring role in a Western that will premiere in a few months, which is a big deal for a guy who had a rough start in life. Although fame comes at a price in Hollywood, at least he's able to escape to Thunder Mountain Ranch and avoid the spotlight for a few days. Or so he thinks, until his attractive and persistent PR rep follows him!

I'm extremely grateful that Harlequin Special Edition has taken on the Thunder Mountain Brotherhood so I can continue to tell stories about these amazing cowboys. It's gonna be a great summer!

Enthusiastically yours,

Vicki Lewis Thompson

In the Cowboy's Arms

———

Vicki Lewis Thompson

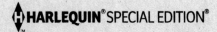

HARLEQUIN® SPECIAL EDITION®

If you purchased this book without a cover you should be aware that this book is stolen property. It was reported as "unsold and destroyed" to the publisher, and neither the author nor the publisher has received any payment for this "stripped book."

Recycling programs
for this product may
not exist in your area.

ISBN-13: 978-0-373-62352-5

In the Cowboy's Arms

Copyright © 2017 by Vicki Lewis Thompson

All rights reserved. Except for use in any review, the reproduction or utilization of this work in whole or in part in any form by any electronic, mechanical or other means, now known or hereinafter invented, including xerography, photocopying and recording, or in any information storage or retrieval system, is forbidden without the written permission of the publisher, Harlequin Enterprises Limited, 225 Duncan Mill Road, Don Mills, Ontario M3B 3K9, Canada.

This is a work of fiction. Names, characters, places and incidents are either the product of the author's imagination or are used fictitiously, and any resemblance to actual persons, living or dead, business establishments, events or locales is entirely coincidental.

This edition published by arrangement with Harlequin Books S.A.

For questions and comments about the quality of this book, please contact us at CustomerService@Harlequin.com.

® and TM are trademarks of Harlequin Enterprises Limited or its corporate affiliates. Trademarks indicated with ® are registered in the United States Patent and Trademark Office, the Canadian Intellectual Property Office and in other countries.

Printed in U.S.A.

www.Harlequin.com

A passion for travel has taken *New York Times* bestselling author **Vicki Lewis Thompson** to Europe, Great Britain, the Greek isles, Australia and New Zealand. She's visited most of North America and has her eye on South America's rain forests. Africa, India and China beckon. But her first love is her home state of Arizona, with its deserts, mountains, sunsets and—last but not least— cowboys! The wide-open spaces and heroes on horseback influence everything she writes. Connect with her at vickilewisthompson.com, Facebook.com/ vickilewisthompson and Twitter.com/vickilthompson.

Books by Vicki Lewis Thompson

Harlequin Blaze

Thunder Mountain Brotherhood

Midnight Thunder
Thunderstruck
Rolling Like Thunder
A Cowboy Under the Mistletoe
Cowboy All Night
Cowboy After Dark
Cowboy Untamed
Cowboy Unwrapped

Sons of Chance

Cowboys & Angels
Riding High
Riding Hard
Riding Home
A Last Chance Christmas

Visit the Author Profile page
at Harlequin.com for more titles.

To Harlequin authors everywhere—

In an uncertain world, our stories have given
pleasure, lightened burdens and changed lives.
We rock.

Chapter One

Broad-shouldered, lean-hipped men with square jaws and captivating eyes were a dime a dozen in Hollywood. After spending all twenty-seven years of her life in Tinseltown, Geena Lysander wasn't easily impressed. It was a testament to the beauty of Matt Forrest that her glasses fogged up whenever he walked into her office.

He was also a decent guy, and she didn't often come across someone who was both ethical and gorgeous. She'd been strongly attracted to him ever since they'd started working together six months ago. Several times she'd caught a flash of heat in his gaze that indicated he had feelings for her, too.

Once she'd thought he'd been ready to ask her out. When he hadn't, she'd decided it was for the best, considering their professional relationship. But that hadn't stopped her from wanting to kiss him, especially when he flashed one of his megawatt smiles.

Judging from the grim set of his mouth, he wouldn't be doing that today. Usually he came in wearing his signature hat, a chocolate-brown Stetson with a turquoise-studded hatband. He favored snug T-shirts, faded jeans and scuffed cowboy boots.

Not this morning. Instead, he'd pulled a generic baseball cap over his thick dark hair and covered his baby blues with aviator shades. He hadn't bothered to shave. She'd never seen that beat-up denim jacket before, either, and he'd turned the collar up even though it was seventy degrees outside. The jeans and the boots were the same, though.

Giving her glasses a quick polish, she smiled, then she put them back on and stood. "Hey."

"Ma'am." He touched the brim of his cap in greeting, but he didn't smile back.

If he'd intended to create a disguise, he'd failed. The paparazzi were experts at spotting celebrities trying to look like street people. And Matt, bless his heart, would look hot as sin no matter what he wore. "Any troubles on the way over?"

He shook his head. "Stayed with a buddy last night, which seems to have thrown them off the trail temporarily. Figured they might be watching my apartment building."

"I can send someone to check that out."

"I appreciate it, but I plan to avoid my place for a while so don't go to any extra trouble." Still no smile, and Matt was the kind of guy who looked for the humor in a situation.

She'd always cherished that about him and hated seeing him so down. He might have exercised poor judgment yesterday, but she understood how that could happen with a costar like Briana Danvers. He was so new at the game. One big-budget movie in the can and another scheduled to start shooting next month meant he was on his way, but he was bound to make a few rookie mistakes in the process.

That's what PR reps like her were for—to repair those little whoopsies.

He took off his shades and stared at her, his gaze bleak. "What now?"

"We'll work through it." As she sat down, she gestured to the chair in front of her desk. "Have a seat."

"Thank you." He lowered his muscular body onto the leather upholstery with a sigh.

"Heard anything from Harvey?" She wasn't crazy about Matt's agent, who headed up a big firm and always seemed to be unavailable or out of the country. But the guy had negotiated the original movie deal and Matt had been signed for another potential blockbuster that would begin filming in a few weeks, so Harvey was getting his client work. That was the bottom line.

"He texted me. Said I should relax, that it would all blow over."

"He's probably right."

"I hope he is, but this has really thrown me for a loop."

"I'm sure it has." And she was determined to help him sort it out, since Harvey had obviously dismissed the issue.

Pulling off his cap, Matt tunneled his fingers through his hair. "I never expected Briana to behave like that or say those things about me." The words were laced with pain.

Geena wondered if she should have seen this train wreck coming and warned him. Briana was seductive, both onscreen and off. The poor guy had probably become lost in the fantasy. "It's easy to develop feelings for a costar. You wouldn't be the first and you won't be the last."

"That's just it. I knew I couldn't let anything happen." He sat forward in his chair, his expression tense. "First of all, she's married, and second, her husband is Clifton effing *Wallace*, everyone's favorite, including my mom's. And mine, actually. He reminds me so much of the Duke."

High praise from Matt. Early on he'd told her that he knew all of John Wayne's movies by heart and repeatedly watched them for inspiration. "It's not the end of the world, Matt. Don't beat yourself up for being human."

"No, ma'am, I'm not." The chair squeaked as he leaned back and gazed at the ceiling. "I'm beating myself up for being stupid. A complete idiot."

Her heart went out to him. Had they not been separated by her desk, she would have squeezed his arm or given him a hug. Then she caught herself imagining that potential hug in far too much detail.

She cleared her throat. "It'll be okay."

"Eventually, I guess." He met her gaze. "I'm sure Harvey has a point. But being called a home wrecker is humiliating. I can take it, but I hate that my folks will have to hear such things."

"They're in Wyoming, right?"

"Yes, ma'am. But they'll have to face their friends and neighbors, and Sheridan's a fairly small town. They've been so proud of me..." His voice trailed off.

"Like I said, we'll handle it. The key is to appear contrite and apologetic. Then I can set you up with some visually appealing charity work, like organizing a benefit for a local animal rescue organization. Fans will overlook this, especially if you seem sufficiently remorseful."

He went very still. "Surely *you* don't believe I hit on her."

"What I think doesn't matter. The media is running a picture of you kissing her outside a café in Burbank. We need to—"

"I didn't kiss her."

"But—"

"*She* kissed *me*."

Judging from the mutual lip-lock Geena had seen in the picture, it was all semantics. "The specific details aren't important. To be honest, getting labeled as a bad boy isn't the worst thing that could happen, especially if we demonstrate that you regret your behavior. Up to now, I've promoted you as Hollywood's fresh new face, a handsome guy with a squeaky clean rep. But fans may like discovering you're not perfect."

His blue eyes lost all expression. "So you think I forced my attentions on Briana."

She would love to believe that he hadn't at least invited that kiss, even if he hadn't initiated it. The pictures were pretty damning. She understood why he wanted to put a different spin on the encounter, but that strategy could backfire into a he-said-she-said nightmare. "It makes no difference who started it. If we jump on the story right away we can take control of the narrative before it gets blown out of proportion."

"I see."

His icy tone made her blink. One glance at his face told her that a wall had gone up. She'd seen that protective shield a couple of times before and had thought the device would serve him well in a brutal business. But employing it against her was counterproductive. "Matt, listen. We can—"

"Sorry, ma'am." He stood and put on his hat and shades. "But I'm outta here."

"Wait!" She leaped up. "You can't leave now. It'll look like you're running away."

"That's fine with me." He turned toward the door.

"Where are you going?"

"Home."

The minute Matt stepped out on the sidewalk they were on him with their cameras, mikes and invasive questions. Must be a slow news day if someone had tracked him over here. Too bad he hadn't called a cab. None were in sight, either.

He shouldered his way through what felt like a mob, but was only five or six reporters, and sprinted toward the nearest bus stop. Three years of running all over town auditioning for commercials had forced him to memorize the public transportation system. There was a bus stop a couple of blocks from here. Thanks to a rigorous training schedule, he was in shape.

He outran the paparazzi and caught the bus right before it pulled away from the curb. After paying the fare he sank gratefully into a seat. Adrenaline plus the blast of A/C made him shiver as he ran through his options.

Going back to his apartment wouldn't work. Even if he made it inside without being accosted, he'd be a virtual prisoner in there until this thing died down. He believed it would. That was what he'd expected Geena to say.

She was a super-smart lady. A little nerdy, but he liked that about her. Tall and slender, she dressed in conservative suits and wore her brown hair up in an arrangement on top of her head. She had a sexy librarian thing going on that had fascinated him from the get-go.

When she was thinking real hard she took off her

glasses and stuck them in her hairdo. He'd envisioned her thinking hard about this mess and coming up with a plan that included hustling him out the back entrance of the building. Then she'd hire a car to spirit him away to some remote cabin in the mountains for a week or so.

He'd even fantasized that she'd take time off and go with him. They could strategize how to deal with this and…yeah, get cozy in the cabin. He'd allowed his brain to come up with an intimate scenario that would never happen, but it had been fun to think about.

Instead, she wanted him to publicly apologize for something he hadn't done and then become proactive by supporting animal rescue. He loved helping a good cause, and animal rescue was dear to his heart. His foster father had devoted his life to a well-respected practice as a large-animal vet.

But Matt balked at using homeless animals as a publicity stunt to prove he was a nice guy. Her plan sucked, but that wasn't the worst part. The real kicker was realizing that Geena believed he'd done what Briana had accused him of.

He felt like ending the relationship with her PR company ASAP, but that was a knee-jerk reaction. He'd give himself time to think about it before doing anything drastic. Aside from being attracted to her, he also liked her and admired that she'd built the company herself. She looked too young to be the head of the firm, and once he'd asked her how old she was. Turned out she was twenty-seven, same as him.

Being near her gave him a buzz, no question, and he'd caught her giving him the eye, too.

He'd debated asking her to dinner to see what might happen. He'd come close to doing it once, but he wasn't sure if asking his PR rep for a date would be an unprofessional move. Making that call wasn't easy in an industry where the lines seemed to blur, but in the end he'd decided to err on the side of caution.

When it came to Briana Danvers, though, his thoughts had been crystal clear. During the filming of *Preston's Revenge* she'd kissed him like she meant it, but he'd never for one second contemplated making a move in private, let alone in a public setting. If Geena thought he had, then she'd seriously misjudged him.

Being blamed for something he didn't do was a hot button. His mom used to do it all the time. Thanks to some counseling, now he could handle the issue if he didn't respect the person doing the judging. But he respected Geena and it bothered him that she thought he could have made a move on Cliff Wallace's wife.

So much for his fantasy of spending a few days in a cabin with her. If she wouldn't help him get the hell out of Dodge, he'd take care of it himself. When he'd told her he was going home, he'd meant Thunder Mountain Ranch where his foster parents lived. They'd saved his bacon when his mom had left him years ago, and ever since then he'd considered them his true family along with his foster brothers.

Rosie and Herb Padgett had been a godsend for many boys caught between a rock and a hard place. But these days, instead of taking in foster kids, they'd opened a residential equine academy for older teens. Much as he wanted to go home, showing up when classes were in session was inconsiderate, especially now that he was a hot item in the scandal sheets.

He used to wonder if he'd ever be famous enough to appear on the cover of the magazines in racks at the grocery store. Thanks to Briana, now he was. They'd plastered that picture everywhere, and one tabloid had dredged up a stock photo of Cliff looking outraged. It'd implied that had been Cliff's reaction. Probably had been, and Matt hated that.

If he could hide out at the ranch for a few days, he wouldn't have to keep seeing those tabloids. A quick check of the Thunder Mountain Academy site on his phone brought good news. The spring session had ended two days ago and summer classes wouldn't start for another week. That meant everyone would be busy preparing the cabins and the rec hall for the next batch of kids.

He could help with that, but first he had to get on a plane. He hadn't paid attention to what bus he'd used to escape the reporters, but this one wouldn't take him to the airport. A few transfers would confuse his pursuers if he still had any, and he could make plane reservations on the way.

His tickets, one to Denver and a separate one on a commuter to the Sheridan County Airport, cost a ridiculous amount. Then again, he was making a ridiculous amount, enough for first class on the LA to Denver leg. He'd considered that briefly, because he didn't fit comfortably in coach, but flying up front would only draw more attention.

Besides, he hated spending money on something so transitory as a bigger seat on the plane. He preferred investing in more permanent pleasures. He'd sunk a good portion of his earnings into a fixer-upper ranch not far from Thunder Mountain. He'd bought it sight unseen as a sanctuary from the craziness of LA, not knowing just how crazy things could get.

Rosie and Herb had checked out the place before he'd signed the papers and they'd assured him it would be beautiful once he gave it some TLC. Although he wouldn't have much time to do that on this trip, he couldn't wait to see it.

Too bad he had to be back in LA so soon, but some publicity gigs for *Preston's Revenge* were scheduled next week, and after that he'd start shooting the new movie. He hoped to God Briana had settled down by the time they had to make a joint appearance. If not, those events would be awkward as hell.

After the relative tranquility of the bus ride, he stepped into the chaos of LAX with trepidation. He scanned the crowd for reporters and then decided he was being paranoid. He wasn't a big enough deal for them to stake out the airport. No one paid attention to him until he had to hand over his driver's license going through security.

The woman's eyes widened. "Aren't you—"

"Yes, ma'am. Please don't react."

"Wouldn't dream of it, honey." She gave him a smile and stamped his boarding pass.

Okay, so maybe not everyone in the world thought he was a scumbag who'd tried to steal Cliff Wallace's wife. In the gate area he spotted several people reading the tabloid that had caused the most commotion because the headline screamed HOME WRECKER in large type. He kept his head down and hoped for the best. A couple of teenage girls snapped some pictures, but he could certainly live with that. Even if they posted them online, the paparazzi couldn't get to him here.

He checked his phone and saw several texts from Geena, although she hadn't tried to call him. He appreciated that. He texted back that he was on his way to Sheridan and would be out of touch for a week or so.

Then it occurred to him he should let Rosie know he was coming. In all the chaos he'd forgotten to do that. She was somewhat psychic, but figuring out he was flying home today might be beyond her powers. He sought out an area that was slightly less noisy and called her.

She answered immediately. "You've been on my mind all morning. How are you, son?"

Her caring voice almost made him lose it. No scolding, no exclamations of horror, no tears. She only wanted to know that he was okay. "I'm fine, Mom. I'm coming home for a few days, if that's okay."

"Of course it's okay! When will you be here?"

He checked his arrival time. "I have a long layover in Denver so I won't make it for dinner. Looks like I'll land about nine or so tonight."

"Cade and Lexi will pick you up."

"Great. Can't wait to see them." His foster brother Cade Gallagher had moved back from Colorado two years ago and reunited with his high school sweetheart, Lexi Simmons. They'd both worked hard to make Thunder Mountain Academy a reality.

"The truck's new, so look for the academy logo on the door. Oh, Matt, I'm so glad you're coming home. I feel the need to see you."

"I feel the need to see you, too." He swallowed a sudden lump in his throat. "Gotta go. We're about to load."

He disconnected and stared at the floor while he pulled himself together. Six months ago he'd called Rosie with the life-changing news that he'd been given the male lead in his first big-budget film. She'd whooped and hollered for a good five minutes before she'd been able to speak rationally.

What a beautiful moment that had been. He'd cherished the idea that she could brag to her friends about her son the movie star. He'd loved giving her something special to celebrate after all she and Herb had done for him. And now that shiny moment had been tarnished.

At least his folks were in Wyoming, far from the ugliness. He never wanted it to touch them. Their privacy meant everything to him and he'd protect it at all costs.

Chapter Two

Matt had no trouble spotting the ranch truck as he stood in the cool night air outside the Sheridan airport waiting for his ride. Cade drove up in a tan, four-door long bed with the Thunder Mountain Academy logo on the door. Lexi wasn't with him, after all, so Matt climbed into the front seat and grasped Cade's outstretched hand.

"Hey, Matt." A straw cowboy hat shadowed Cade's face, but his subdued greeting telegraphed his concern. "No luggage?"

"Nope." Matt closed the door and fastened his seat belt.

"At least you stayed ahead of the peasants with the pitchforks." Cade put the truck in gear and pulled out.

"Barely. Nice truck."

"Mom likes me to drive it whenever I come to town. She thinks it's good for the academy's image."

Matt leaned back against the seat. "Yeah, until some derelict gets in."

"Now that you mention it, you do look a little rough around the edges, bro. Is the scruff for your next role?"

"The scruff is for lack of a razor, although I figured it also might keep people from recognizing me."

"Oh."

"So, where's Lexi?"

"She thought we might need some brotherhood moments so she's waiting at the ranch with Mom and Dad."

"Wow." Lexi's understanding touched him. "That's... really nice of her."

"That's my lady. She has it all going on."

"You're a lucky guy."

"Yes, yes, I am." Cade stopped at a red light and took a deep breath. "And since she's given us the chance to talk, let me say this whole thing bites. I mean, one damn kiss. It's not like you were boinking that woman in the middle of Sunset Boulevard. And wouldn't you know some jackass would be there with a camera."

"Of course he was." In spite of his exhaustion, Matt's anger flared to life. "She hired him to be there."

"What?"

"She set me up." Matt's stomach clenched as he said it out loud for the first time. "I can't prove it yet, but the long layover in Denver allowed me to think through all that's happened and I've put the pieces together. I realize everything started on the last day of shooting when she propositioned me."

"Aw, hell. Seriously?"

"Afraid so. I've never told anyone about it, though, so keep it to yourself."

"Goes without saying."

"Anyway, she was a little drunk, but not that drunk. She said Cliff wasn't man enough for her anymore."

"Anymore? They've been married for like three years, tops!"

Matt shrugged. "Who knows what their relationship is like? She promised we'd be discreet and no one would ever have to know. I turned her down as nicely as I could, but—"

"Now she hates you with the heat of a thousand branding irons."

"Sure looks that way. She invited me to lunch yesterday, supposedly to apologize for her inappropriate behavior. Instead, she kissed me in front of witnesses and then told the media I was the aggressor."

"Holy shit on a swizzle stick."

"Yeah." He glanced over at Cade. "But now that I'm out of paparazzi range it should die down. Without me to harass they'll focus on some other poor slob. At least, that's my plan. And I'd like to forget Briana Danvers while I'm here, so let's talk about something else. You still have that gray tabby cat?"

"You remember Ringo?"

"Absolutely. He was one of the highlights from that quick visit last year."

Cade chuckled. "Ringo's living the life. Ever since Lexi moved into my cabin he prefers staying there with us instead of patrolling the barn looking for mice. He's turned into a feline couch potato."

"Smart cat."

"Smarter than we are, that's for sure. Listen, you may want to forget about Briana, but I'm just getting started thinking about her and I want justice." Cade smacked the steering wheel. "Here's an idea! We'll call a press conference so you can tell your side. We can't let her get away with this crap."

His brother had his back. The heaviness lifted from Matt's shoulders and he smiled for the first time in twenty-four hours. A press conference in Sheridan, Wyoming. That would be a first, especially if they could get any members of the press to show up, which wasn't likely.

"I don't know how to organize a press conference," Cade continued, "but I'll bet you do. Or you know people who know people. We can make it happen."

"Look, it's a good impulse and I appreciate the moral support, but a press conference won't work for a lot of reasons."

"What she's done is *wrong*, damn it! It's character assassination and you need to defend yourself."

"I doubt I can. She's a very good actress who knows her camera angles. She orchestrated that kiss so I'd look guilty as charged. Even if I try to tell my side, hardly anyone will believe me."

"They might if you tell them about the proposition."

"Not doing that."

Cade groaned. "I should have known you wouldn't. You're too noble for your own good, buddy. She doesn't deserve your overdeveloped sense of chivalry."

"It's not her I'm thinking about. It's Cliff Wallace. I respect the hell out of the guy. He has lousy instincts when it comes to women, but like I said, Briana's a very good actress. He may eventually find out the truth about her, but not because of me."

"You had some love scenes with her, right?"

"Oh, yeah."

"Hot?"

"Yep."

Cade was silent for a while. Then he cleared his throat.

"Let me just say I respect the hell out of *you*, cowboy. A lot of guys would have taken her up on that offer."

"Not if they were members of the Thunder Mountain Brotherhood." Matt took great pride in being a part of the group Cade had started years ago with Damon Harrison and Finn O'Roarke, the first three foster boys. Now every guy who'd lived at the ranch was included.

"True."

"And not if they'd been raised by Herb and Rosie."

Cade grinned. "Also true. And for the record, Mom's been informing everyone that the tabloids got it wrong. You never would have behaved that way."

"God, I love that woman."

"Don't we all." He looked over at Matt. "Are you planning to tell her everything you just told me?"

"Probably not."

"I wouldn't, either, unless you want her to buy a ticket to LA and open up a can of whoop-ass on Briana. She's already put a couple of DVDs in the trash compactor."

Matt chuckled at the image of Rosie listening to the crunch as the DVDs bit the dust. "That's why I had to come home, so I could hear stuff like this. Mom's destroying DVDs and you're ready to call a press conference. It's a far better reaction than what I got from my PR rep this morning."

"Which was?"

"She wanted me to publicly show remorse for my behavior."

Cade met that comment with several choice swear words. "So, did you fire her?"

"Not yet. She doesn't know me that well and the photo convinced her I'd forced myself on Briana."

"Did you tell her you hadn't?"

"Yeah, I said it was the other way around—that Briana kissed me—but Geena didn't think it mattered who kissed who. I'm supposed to suck it up and be apologetic."

"That's her name? Geena?"

"Geena Lysander."

"Well, this Geena person should have believed you. She should have taken your side. Apologize, my ass."

"In a way, she was trying to take my side. She kept telling me it would be okay and we'd fix this." He thought of the earnest light in her eyes as she'd laid out her plan. She had pretty eyes, and when they took on that special gleam, he had the urge to kiss her. Like that would ever happen.

"Well, you're not apologizing."

"Nope. I'll just hide out for the next few days. My phone's been off for hours and I'm growing fond of that mode. I might leave it off."

"But you're a big-deal actor now. Don't you have to stay in touch with your peeps?"

"My peeps are all right here in Sheridan. You, Lexi, Rosie and Herb. Plus Damon and Philomena. How's their baby doing, by the way?"

"Sophie's cute as hell, bright red hair just like her mother's. And Jake Ramsey moved back to town. He's working at the fire station and engaged to Amethyst Ferguson. Remember her?"

Matt laughed. "Doesn't everybody? I can't hear 'Santa Baby' without remembering her sexy performance back in high school. I thought she'd be giving Taylor Swift a run for her money by now."

"Turns out she'd rather stick to performing locally."

"You know, after what just happened, I get that."

"Please don't tell me you're hanging it up because of this nonsense."

"No, I'm not. I'm starting a new movie next month."

"Awesome! I don't think I heard about that."

"It came up pretty fast, and I kept meaning to call Mom but then this thing hit." Matt let out a weary sigh. "But I'll hang in there. I love acting. Always have."

"The ultimate escape." Cade glanced at him. "Do you remember telling me that?"

"I do, actually. School plays were great when I was a kid, but this...you can completely disappear into the role. You don't have to worry about what to say because they hand you a script. You don't have to wonder how everything will turn out, either. It's all written out."

"Sounds damned appealing. It's a wonder more of us didn't get into that line of work. Perfect way to forget about things you'd rather not remember."

"Sure is. But I need a break. I'm ready to unplug, at least for the next week or so. Let's talk about your wedding. Third weekend in August, right?"

"Yep."

"I want all the deets, bridegroom."

"You won't be bored?"

"Not a chance." He settled back, ready to hear about something positive for a change.

Once Cade got started on the subject of his upcoming nuptials, he barely stopped for breath. Matt got a kick out of his excitement. By the time they turned down the dirt road leading to the ranch, the humiliation of the past twenty-four hours seemed unimportant compared to Cade's obvious joy in marrying the love of his life.

The tabloid blitz had loomed large back in LA, but moonlight shining on the massive bulk of the Bighorns put everything in perspective. Cade parked in the circular gravel drive in front of the low-slung ranch house and Matt swung down from the cab. Lamplight coming through the windows allowed him to see Rosie, Herb and Lexi sitting in the Adirondack chairs lined up on the long porch.

They called out a greeting as they started down the steps. Matt hadn't shaved or showered in two days, but nobody seemed to care. Arms outstretched, they gathered him close. Coming home had been the right thing to do.

As the crow flew, Sheridan didn't seem that far from LA. Geena wished she could get there by crow, because clearly traveling by passenger plane would take all flipping day. The layover in Denver was ridiculous, but it gave her plenty of time to think about where she'd gone wrong with Matt Forrest.

And she'd gone very wrong with him. She'd also under-estimated Briana Danvers's thirst for publicity. Somehow the woman had learned that Matt had left town and she'd made a huge deal of it, calling his departure an admission of guilt.

That was exactly why Geena had wanted him to stick around, but she'd handled the situation poorly. Because she'd dealt with her fair share of clients caught in compromising situations off the set, she'd assumed Matt fell into that category. She'd expected him to agree with her plan to contain the damage. Instead, he'd stormed out of her office.

So she'd gone into research mode. A friend had sent her the dailies from *Preston's Revenge*. The scenes between Briana and Matt were off the charts, but did that mean he'd aggressively pursued her?

She was less and less sure about that. Briana was married to a revered but aging Western movie star. What if she'd been captivated by Matt? He claimed that she'd initiated the kiss.

And, unlike other clients, he seemed horrified by the

drama that photo had created. Some stars were thrilled by any publicity at all, even if it was potentially negative. Not Matt. He'd chosen to hide out.

It might have been a workable strategy except that Briana obviously planned to keep stirring the pot. Matt needed to fight back or he was liable to be forever labeled with Briana's taunt of *run, Forrest, run*.

No other celebrities were doing something stupid this week, so the gossip mags were hungry for anything Briana fed them. The situation reflected poorly on Geena's firm, which she'd started only three years ago, but that wasn't why she'd decided to make a trip to Sheridan. She couldn't bear to stand by and watch Matt take a beating.

So she'd booked her flights to Sheridan, a place that was not easy to get to. But she'd brave a puddle jumper if that's what it took to talk to Matt face-to-face.

He wouldn't be happy to see his PR rep, though. She reminded herself of that as she drove her rented SUV down some of the darkest roads she'd ever seen. Thank God for her GPS or she'd surely have ended up in some pasture staring at an angry bull.

She almost missed the turnoff to Thunder Mountain Ranch. At the last minute she saw it, thanks to a small spotlight trained on the carved wooden sign. A second sign hung below it proclaiming this the *Home of Thunder Mountain Academy*.

She had no idea what that was about, but the ranch was listed as Matt's home address so she'd forge on. Presumably his parents, Rosie and Herb Padgett, lived here. He'd probably changed his last name to something less jarring than Matt Padgett, which was smart marketing.

The dirt road leading to the ranch was even darker than the highway. If she'd spent the night in Sheridan, she could have tackled this road first thing in the morning. But Matt would have an easier time turning her away in broad daylight. A gentleman didn't send a lady back out into the night after she'd traveled all day to see him. And Matt Forrest was a gentleman.

She'd allowed the turmoil Briana had created to obscure that basic fact. Briana might be irresistible to the majority of males out there, but despite her famous allure, Matt would never succumb to it in a public place. Such behavior would have violated his personal code of conduct, one that probably had its roots right here on this extremely authentic-looking ranch and in all the John Wayne movies he'd memorized.

Arriving unannounced with a small overnight case in the passenger seat was cheeky. She planned to leave it there and see what happened after she knocked on the door, but in movies ranch houses always had spare bedrooms. Staying in the same house as Matt would help the cause, since she didn't expect instant cooperation.

The SUV's tires crunched on a layer of thick gravel as she navigated the circular drive and parked by the front door. Hers was the only vehicle there, but several more were down by a large hip-roofed barn. The Adirondack chairs lined up on the long front porch were empty, but when she stepped out of the car, she heard country music coming from the house. And laughter, both male and female. It seemed she'd arrived in the middle of a party.

Well, that made sense. His folks had probably decided to celebrate his success and ignore the scandal. No wonder he'd wanted to come back to that kind of love and support.

She paused beside the SUV. Her arrival would be about as popular as Maleficent crashing a baby shower. On the other hand, having lots of people around might be a good thing. She was fine with crowds. Growing up with a Hollywood star for a mom, she'd learned to handle herself in any circumstance, no matter how bizarre or awkward.

She was still debating what to do when the front door opened and a redheaded woman came out holding a baby who looked to be about five or six months old. A tall guy tugged on the brim of his cowboy hat as he followed her out and started to close the door.

"I still say she said my name," called someone from inside, someone who sounded a lot like Matt.

Laughing, the cowboy swung the door open again. "You're dreaming, bro!" he called back.

"Aw, come on, Damon." The redhead was busy fiddling with the baby's blanket and obviously hadn't spotted the SUV yet. "Let Uncle Matt have his little fantasy."

"You heard her," the guy named Damon said as he closed the door. "She was saying *ma-ma* like she always does. She—hello, who's this?" He put a protective hand on the woman's shoulder and looked in Geena's direction.

She moved away from the vehicle and came toward them. "My name's Geena Lysander and I'm here to see Matt Forrest, but apparently I'm interrupting a celebration."

"Geena Lysander," the woman said. "Your name came up tonight. Aren't you his PR rep?"

"Yes, and I'm here to discuss—"

"Let me stop you right there, ma'am." The tall cowboy descended the steps. "From what I understand, he's not interested in having any more discussions. He came here to get away from all that, so I'm afraid you've made a trip for nothing. My wife and I can lead you back into town and get you settled in a hotel room, though."

Despite Geena's height, augmented by four-inch heels, she had to look up to meet his determined gaze. Judging from the set of his jaw, he planned to do whatever was necessary to keep her from going up to the front door. Clearly he intended to protect Matt from the likes of her.

As she debated her next move, the door opened again and Matt stepped out holding a pacifier. At first he looked confused by her presence, but gradually his expression hardened into a mask of anger.

She despaired of getting through to him but she had to try. "I realize you're not happy to see me."

"No, ma'am, I'm not."

"But we need to talk."

Instead of responding to her comment, he gestured to the SUV. "Is that your vehicle?"

"Yes. I rented it."

"No worries, bro," Damon said. "We'll lead her back to town and help her find a hotel room."

Matt shook his head. "I appreciate the offer, but this is my deal and I'll handle the problem." He gave the pacifier to the redhead. "Found this on the sofa and thought you might need it. You two head on home with Sophie. I'll grab the keys to the ranch truck and make sure Geena has a place for the night." He glanced over at her. "And a plane reservation in the morning."

"We're not in a rush," Damon said. "We'll hang out here until you fetch the truck keys."

"Listen, you don't have to stand guard over me." Geena glanced toward the baby, who was starting to fuss. "I promise to stay right here while Matt gets those keys. I'm sure you'd like to get home."

"We would. Sophie's hungry." The redhead jiggled the bundle in her arms. "I think you can stand down, cowboy. Geena doesn't look dangerous."

"Okay." Damon faced Geena and touched the brim of his hat in farewell. "Ma'am."

"Bye." She felt wistful as she watched them walk toward the vehicles parked near the barn. She couldn't remember a time when anyone had stood between her and a potential threat. Must be nice.

Chapter Three

Geena had solid brass ones. Matt would give her that much, but nothing else. She'd made it as far as the driveway, but she wasn't coming any closer than that. Once he'd escorted her to a hotel in town, he'd fire her like he should have done yesterday. Then she'd have to fly home because she wouldn't have any reason to hang around.

He stepped inside the house and paused to take a calming breath. Barreling in looking agitated would provoke a bunch of questions. He'd like to do this with as little discussion as possible. He'd already talked about the subject more than he wanted to.

During dinner Phil had asked whether he had publicity folks doing damage control and he'd described his meeting with Geena. He wasn't surprised that Damon had been ready to escort her straight back to town, but that wasn't his responsibility or Phil's.

The living room furniture had been moved aside for

dancing, and now that Damon and Phil had left, only four people occupied the floor. Cade and Lexi were teaching some elaborate new move to Herb and Rosie. Matt hated to break that up, but it couldn't be helped.

As he approached the group, Cade glanced at him. "How about you partner with Lexi? I know this already."

"I'd be glad to, but I have a little errand to run. Can I borrow the ranch truck for a couple of hours?"

Herb looked puzzled. "Certainly, but I can't imagine what sort of errand you'd have to run at this hour."

"Don't pry," Rosie said. "Maybe he's heard from an old girlfriend."

Cade nudged back his hat. "That would be a trick, since he made such a huge deal about turning off his phone for the next week." His voice softened. "What's up, bro?"

"We have an uninvited guest and I need to escort her back to town."

Rosie blinked. "A woman's outside? Did some star-struck fan follow you here?"

"No, she's not a fan. Look, if it's okay, I'll just get the keys and take care of this."

"Hang on," Cade said. "If it's some damned reporter, let me go out there with you. I'm sure between the two of us we can convince her to get lost."

Matt sighed. He probably should have spit it out in the beginning. "She's not a reporter, either. It's Geena. If I can borrow the truck for a couple of hours, I'll—"

"Great." Cade started for the door. "I'm delighted she's here and she's not going anywhere until I've told her exactly what I think of how she treated you."

"No!" Matt blocked Cade's progress. "Nobody's going out there except me. All I need is the keys to the truck. She doesn't know the area so I feel an obligation to make sure she gets back to town okay and has a hotel room. Then I'll make damn sure she knows that she has to leave in the morning."

"Matt." Rosie sent him a look of reproach. "The woman traveled all the way from Los Angeles to see you. I realize you're annoyed with her, but shooing her away after she's made that kind of effort isn't good manners."

He stared at his foster mother. "She showed up uninvited. That isn't good manners, either."

"True, but two wrongs don't make a right. Sending her back where she came from might give you temporary satisfaction, but it's not the gracious thing to do."

"But—"

"Is she an evil person?"

"No."

"Has she deliberately harmed you in any way?"

Matt sighed. He'd lived with Rosie long enough to know where this was going. "No."

"Then you need to take the high road, son. Invite her to join us and I'll offer to put her up."

Every instinct told him that this was a bad idea. "I don't want her here, Mom." He clenched both fists. "Whatever nastiness happened in LA stays in LA. I don't want you and Dad involved. Or anyone in my family, for that matter."

Rosie studied him for a moment. "I understand that and I appreciate your desire to protect us. That's very gallant. I can tell you're very angry that she's come here, but let's think about why she did. Her job is to make you look good, right?"

"Supposedly, but I don't like her plan or the fact she came to my home uninvited. I'm going to fire her."

"Do you have a replacement lined up?"

"Not yet."

"Considering you need a PR person to guide you through this incident, you might want to hold off ditching the one you have. I agree that you shouldn't apologize for something you didn't do, but she's on your turf now." Rosie smiled. "You don't agree with her plan for handling things, but now you have a golden opportunity to change her mind."

Cade nodded, a gleam in his eyes. "And I have a golden opportunity to give her a piece of mine. Yeah, let's invite her in. Can't wait."

"Cade Gallagher." Rosie pinned him with her gaze. "You will not ambush someone who's a guest in this house. In fact, I'm going out there to issue the invitation myself. You boys stay right here. And once she walks through that door, you'll be on your best behavior with her at all times. Is that clear?"

"Yes, ma'am," Matt and Cade said in unison.

Lexi's muffled snort was the only sound in the room as Rosie turned and left.

Geena reasoned that she hadn't completely lost out. Matt was enough of a gentleman to make sure she found her way back to Sheridan and that she had a place to stay. While she could handle everything herself, she'd accept his help because it would give her a chance to accomplish what she'd come for.

Sometime during their interaction she'd apologize for assuming he'd accosted Briana. Then she'd make her case for having him come back to repair the damage to his reputation. Grabbing a few moments on the fly wasn't ideal, but at least her trip wouldn't be completely wasted.

God, he'd been angry, so angry that his blue eyes had glittered like a pair of Fourth of July sparklers. The effect had been thrilling, actually, seeing him go into protec-

tor mode concerning his home and family. Now wasn't
a good time to think about it, but that cowboy turned
her on.

When the front door opened she expected him to come
out bringing all his Matt Forrestness with him.

Instead, a plump woman with blond hair walked out
on the porch and down the steps. She approached and
held out her hand. "Hello, Geena. I'm Rosie Padgett,
Matt's foster mom."

"Foster mom?" Geena heard herself and cringed.
"Sorry, that was rude." She accepted Rosie's firm hand-
shake. "It's just that from the way Matt talked about you,
I thought he was your son."

"He is. They all are. Many years ago Herb and I started
taking in boys with nowhere else to go. Most of them
ended up calling us Mom and Dad, which pleases us no
end. We couldn't have kids of our own and now we're
blessed with a huge family. We love it."

"Wow. So this ranch used to be a foster home?"

"Sure did, although once again, the boys usually
dropped the word *foster* after they'd been here awhile.
The ranch was just home."

"That's wonderful." She was beginning to realize how
little she knew about Matt. But she doubted Rosie had
walked out here to give her a quick history lesson.

"It has been. Listen, I know you've had a long trip.
I'll bet you could use some food and something to drink.
Why don't you come in?"

Whoa. Talk about falling down the rabbit hole. "Uh,
because Matt doesn't want me to?"

"You're right, he doesn't. He's embarrassed about the
mess with Briana Danvers and hates how it's affected his
life. He made the trip without going back to his apartment because he didn't want to be waylaid. He asked

me to shop for him today so he'd have a few clothes and some toiletries."

"Poor guy."

"He's hurting, that's for sure. And he doesn't want any of it touching his family." Rosie paused. "But unless you have paparazzi hiding in your SUV, I can't imagine how bringing you inside would involve us in the scandal."

"I promise I'm not dragging a gaggle of reporters behind me. Sheridan isn't the easiest place in the world to access by air. Matt's not a big enough story to warrant suffering through long layovers and tiny planes."

Rosie laughed. "I love that about this town. But in spite of the inconvenience, here you are."

"Because I really have to talk to him."

"I'm sure you do. Just because Matt doesn't go online doesn't mean I haven't. I've sent that woman an email letting her know what I think of her shenanigans, not that she'll ever see it."

"No, she probably won't. I'm sure her PR people filter out the negative ones. I do the same for my clients. If I thought this would go away I'd ignore her, but she's escalated the attack. That's why I need to discuss it with Matt."

"Then let's make that happen. You're lucky we were having a party or we all might have been in bed."

"Oh! I didn't think of that!"

"I'll bet nobody goes to bed at ten in Los Angeles."

"Not anyone I know. Plus it's an hour earlier there. I forgot about the time change, which isn't like me. I apologize."

"As it turns out, it doesn't matter. But I should warn you that ranch folks get up at dawn so we don't tend to be night owls unless it's a special occasion."

"Then I won't stay long. And I really don't need someone to lead me back to town and find me a hotel. I can manage."

"No reason for you to do that. We have plenty of room."

Geena was stunned. "You're suggesting I stay here?"

"I am."

"I don't think that's a good idea."

"Actually, it's a fine idea. I assume you have a bag with you?"

"Yes, but—"

"Then let's get it." Rosie started toward the SUV.

"Wait a minute. Matt will hit the roof. I knew he'd be upset but I had no idea how upset. After I talk with him I'll drive into town like he suggested. I don't want to cause problems."

"Trust me, there will be no problems."

"You're sure?"

"Absolutely sure." Rosie opened the passenger door and reached for the overnight bag.

"Oh, no, let me get it." Geena edged her out of the way. "It's bad enough that I arrived unannounced and uninvited. I won't have you schlepping my luggage." She pulled out the small carry-on and closed the door.

"The way I figure it," Rosie said as they started back toward the porch, "you came unannounced because you had to. If you'd told Matt, he would have met you at the airport and sent you right back."

"Guaranteed."

"I realize there's a crisis here, and it's a shame you and Matt don't see eye-to-eye on how it should be managed."

"Yes, it is."

"Just so you're clear on my position, I agree with him that he shouldn't have to make a public apology. He didn't do anything wrong."

"I know that now." Geena lifted her bag so it would clear the steps. "It's one of the things I want to tell him."

Rosie glanced over, her expression eager. "You have proof?"

"Unfortunately not. But when I started thinking about what a gentleman he is, I knew he wouldn't have deliberately embarrassed a woman in public."

"Ah. That's a good start. You're beginning to see who he is under the pretty packaging."

Geena choked on a laugh. "Excuse me?"

"Don't tell me you haven't noticed that he's a beautiful young man, because I won't believe you."

"Okay, I've noticed."

"I'm sure that Briana noticed, too. I have a feeling we don't have the whole story, but like you said, Matt's a gentleman. We might have to get the info out of Cade."

"Cade?"

"One of Matt's brothers. He's inside with his fiancée, Lexi, so you'll get to meet both of them, plus my husband, Herb. This is all working out for the best." She opened the door. "After you."

A knot of anxiety settled in Geena's stomach as she walked into the living room carrying her overnight bag. Sure, she was good at handling awkward situations in the world of glitz and glamour. Somehow it was easier when a large number of the participants had an agenda, often a self-serving one.

She hadn't spent much time around people who weren't jockeying for a spot on the next rung up, people who got up at dawn to feed the chickens or whatever it was they found to do at that hour. She'd never set foot on an honest-to-God ranch, let alone a ranch that used to be a foster home.

Had she ever known someone who'd been a foster kid?

If so, they hadn't told her about it. Matt hadn't told her, either. He'd obviously considered it private information and she respected that.

The comfy-looking living room furniture had been shoved against the wall, probably to create a dance floor. Even without a fire in the fireplace, the room had a cozy, lived-in feel. She could imagine how much it would appeal to a homeless boy.

The good-looking, dark-haired cowboy standing next to a woman with short brown curls had to be Cade, the one most likely to have the inside scoop on what had gone down between Matt and Briana. The woman must be Lexi, who fit right into the casual setting in her jeans, boots and long-sleeved yellow T-shirt.

Cade wore a cowboy hat indoors, like Matt always did. Apparently that was the custom around here, although the older gentleman wasn't wearing one. She pegged him as Herb, Rosie's husband.

For one awful moment there was total silence in the room. It made her realize that the heels, nifty black jacket and pencil skirt she'd worn on the plane were out of place on a working ranch, but she didn't own Western wear and she'd wanted to look professional.

Matt was the first to move. "Let me take that." He came forward and divested her of the bag.

"Thank you."

He gave her a curt nod. "You're welcome. Mom, where should I put it?"

"The green bedroom's all made up."

"Right." He disappeared down a hallway.

"Hi, Geena." Lexi walked over to shake her hand. "I'm Lexi Simmons and this is my fiancé, Cade Gallagher."

Cade touched the brim of his hat. "Ma'am." The greeting, polite but with no warmth, was identical to the fare-well Damon had given her a while ago.

"I'm Herb, Rosie's husband." The wiry guy had kind eyes and a firm grip. "Welcome to Thunder Mountain."

"Thank you." She swallowed a lump of nervousness. "I'm glad to be here."

"And we're pleased to have you." Rosie said it as if daring anyone to contradict her.

Geena couldn't remember when she'd felt less sure of herself. "Look, you were all doing something before I barged in here, so please continue."

"We were working on a dance step," Lexi said. "I don't suppose you'd want to learn—"

"Why not?" Geena nudged off her heels and put them in a corner.

"Before you get into that," Rosie said, "are you hungry? Can I make you a sandwich?"

"I'm starving." Her hunger pangs wouldn't allow her to say anything but the truth. "I headed out here as soon as I picked up the rental." Her gaze swept the room. "I knew it was late, although I didn't realize how late. I apologize for that."

"Then let me fix you something. Any issues? Food allergies?"

"I'll be grateful for anything, but let me make it myself. I don't expect to be waited on."

Rosie waved her off. "Tomorrow I'll put you to work, but tonight relax and enjoy yourself. What do you want to drink?"

"Water, please."

"That's it? How about an adult beverage?"

Geena considered where she was and what they might have on hand. Under the circumstances, alcohol would be welcome. "A beer would be great."

Matt came back at that moment. "I'll get it. You can sample my brother's brew." He said it with enormous pride before leaving the room.

"Cade?" She glanced to him. "You make beer?"

"Oh, no, not me. That would be Finn O'Roarke. He has a microbrewery in Seattle. Very successful." His gaze issued a challenge. "We have a lot of talent in the brotherhood. Brewers, lawyers, horse trainers, firefighters. You name it, we got it."

"Impressive. You called it a *brotherhood*. What's that all about?"

"Nothing." Matt arrived and handed her an open bottle of beer and a glass before turning to glare at Cade. "Absolutely nothing."

"Yeah." Cade exchanged a glance with Matt. "Just a figure of speech. Not important."

Geena didn't push it, but her PR instincts were telling her that if Matt belonged to a group calling themselves *the brotherhood*, she needed to pay attention. A public apology for the kiss didn't interest her anymore, now that she knew Matt would have to lie in order to make one. But apparently he had a rich tradition of family and loyalty.

She could work the heck out of that angle. Fans would love to know that he was part of a close-knit group of foster brothers who'd grown up on a working ranch. Talk about wholesome. She wasn't sure what would be the best promo vehicle to get the story out, but it probably didn't matter. Judging from his reaction so far, he'd never let that story be told.

Chapter Four

Matt hadn't wanted Geena anywhere near his family, and yet here she was, and damned if she didn't fit in much better than he could have predicted. Barefoot and wearing a tight skirt that restricted her movements, she still managed to execute the dance moves Cade and Lexi taught her.

Worse yet, she was very appealing doing it. No, not just appealing. The glasses paired with her excellent sense of rhythm created a dynamite combination of brains and sexy moves.

In the months he'd known Geena he'd had many inappropriate thoughts about her, even though mostly she'd sat behind her desk while they talked. She wasn't behind her desk now, and every time she wiggled her hips, his johnson gave a twitch in response.

She was making inroads with his family members, too. His mom had defected immediately and he wanted to know what those two had talked about outside. Lexi and Herb had both warmed to her, as well. Cade had been a holdout for quite a while, but her willingness to learn the new dance step was slowly winning him over.

Then Rosie brought in Geena's sandwich and everyone took a break. Matt fetched some chips and more of Finn's beer from the fridge in the rec room. That was another thing. Earlier, Geena had put down the glass he'd brought her and was drinking from the bottle like everyone else. It was a small thing, but small things added up. She was easy to be with.

While Geena ate, the group lounged on the displaced furniture and talked about Thunder Mountain Academy. Matt hadn't wanted Geena to know anything about that, either, but it was a logical topic because several chores were in the works during this break between sessions.

Geena seemed fascinated by every aspect of the program. Matt's family softened even more in response to her enthusiasm. It wasn't artificial enthusiasm, either. That was a quality he'd liked about her from the beginning. Hollywood was crawling with fakes, but Geena never pretended to be something she wasn't.

Perfect example—she could have arrived all duded up in an effort to present herself as a cowgirl. Instead, she'd worn the type of clothes he'd always seen her in. This was his first glimpse of her bare toes, however. She'd propped her feet up on the coffee table and he couldn't help noticing her sea-blue polish. And her delicate ankles and shapely calves.

He looked away. The situation was complicated enough already.

"Do you ride?" Lexi asked her.

"I don't know the first thing about horses." Geena finished off her sandwich. "I take that back. I know what a Clydesdale is because I've seen the commercials. My hat's off to whoever came up with the idea of using them to market beer."

Lexi smiled. "Yeah, everybody loves those big ol' horses, me included. I just thought you might be a rider since you're so interested in the academy."

"I wouldn't mind trying it sometime, but I'd be a total beginner."

"Want to try it while you're here?"

Matt bit back a groan. That was so Lexi, eager to introduce the uninitiated to the wonders of horseback riding. That was why she was such a good teacher, but in this case he wished she'd zip her lip.

"I'd love to, but all I brought to wear was stuff like this." Geena gestured to her skirt and jacket.

"I can find you some clothes and boots," Rosie said. "I've stocked up on spare items for the students."

"I don't know. I'm pretty tall."

"So are some of the girls we get here. I try to be prepared when pants get ripped and kids come with expensive boots that shouldn't be worn to muck out stalls."

"So they have to be financially well-off to attend?"

"At first they did." Herb hadn't spoken much but this was a favorite topic of his. "We're working on changing that. We already have one scholarship opportunity thanks to Ben Radcliffe, a local saddle maker who conducts a class every semester. We're looking for more sponsors. There are plenty of kids who would benefit but don't have the tuition."

"I'll offer a scholarship," Matt said. "I can probably handle two or three if the money stays good. I can't believe I haven't thought of it before."

"That's brilliant." Geena smiled. "Too bad we can't

get it organized this week because a picture of you with a recipient would be—"

"Not happening." Matt gazed at her and wished they didn't always have to be on opposite sides of this particular fence. But she didn't seem to get his need for privacy. Maybe he'd have to fire her, after all. "The scholarships would be anonymous."

She frowned. "You'd be throwing away a great PR opportunity if you do that."

"And keeping my personal life separate from my public one. That's always been important to me, but after what happened two days ago, it's critical."

Her shoulders slumped. "That makes it tough to do my job."

"I know. But that's the way it has to be."

"It's okay. I'll think of something else. I—" She stifled a yawn. "Sorry. It's been a long day. I guess the beer and food made me sleepy."

"I'm sure you're exhausted." Rosie switched into mothering mode. "You should get some rest. I know what I said about getting up at dawn, but you don't have to."

"Oh, no, I want to." She glanced at the grandfather clock in the corner. "When is dawn, anyway?"

That got a laugh. Even Matt couldn't help grinning. She was such a city girl. But she was also game for anything, which meant she'd get along fine in this new setting. Resilience was a valued commodity around here.

"It's around five fifteen," his dad said.

Her eyes widened. "That early?"

"But you don't have to get up then," Herb continued. "We do because the horses need to be fed and turned out to pasture. Rosie likes to organize the food for breakfast, but we don't eat until after six, so you'll have some extra time to ease into the day."

"Well, um, I never eat breakfast."

"You'll want to eat this one." Lexi glanced over at Cade. "Nobody fixes a better breakfast than Rosie. Am I right?"

"Except for you, sweetheart."

"Nice try, Gallagher." Lexi gave him an affectionate nudge. "Flattery will get you nowhere. You're still responsible for fifty percent of the cooking at our house."

Cade sighed. "But I'm still no good at it."

"You're improving. That's what's important."

"You're both invited down here in the morning, though," Rosie said. "It's not every day we see Matt at the breakfast table. But Geena, you're excused. I'll have the coffeepot on until at least eight, so if that's all you need, come in and help yourself. We don't force food on anyone."

"I'll be there at six and I'd love to have your breakfast. I'll also get up at dawn to watch Herb feed the horses. I've never seen anybody do that except in the movies."

Herb smiled. "It's not all that exciting."

"Maybe not to you, because you do it every day. Me, I get up, get dressed, hit the drive-through at Starbucks and head to my office. Feeding horses at five thirty in the morning is exotic."

"Then you're welcome to show up at dawn."

"Great. Thank you." She turned to Matt. "Listen, before I toddle off to bed, can I have a word with you?"

His mom stood. "We can leave you two alone so you can talk."

"Heavens, no! You're all settled in. Matt and I will step out onto the porch." She glanced at him. "Okay with you?"

"Sure." He shouldn't have had that last beer. He was feeling way too mellow and he had to stay sharp. But refusing to have a chat on the porch would seem rude and his mom would call him on it.

Geena walked out there barefoot and that charmed him. He didn't want to be charmed any more than he wanted to have sexy thoughts about her. He needed to be tough and uncompromising as he sought to protect his family from…he was no longer clear what that was. He hadn't wanted any part of his life in LA to intrude on his life here, and yet Geena had inserted herself into his inner circle and the sky hadn't fallen.

After he closed the door, she turned and leaned her slim hips against the porch railing. She looked tired, which was understandable. The trip from California was taxing, especially for someone who wasn't used to long layovers, little planes and country roads. She'd probably fare better traveling to New York or London than making her way to Sheridan, Wyoming, home to folks who climbed out of bed at the crack of dawn.

He found a spot to lean against the front wall of the house so they'd both be standing. He suspected she hadn't taken one of the Adirondack chairs because she doubted she'd have the energy to pull herself back out of it. A cricket chirped nearby and a breeze stirred the tall pines not far from the house.

Geena sighed. "This is nice."

"Yeah." A little too nice. Even though his family was just beyond that door, he knew they wouldn't come out. They understood this was private

That left him with a feeling of intimacy he'd never experienced with Geena. They were truly alone for the first time since she'd arrived. He began thinking about how she'd feel in his arms and how her lips would taste. Did she have a lover? After watching her dance, he could easily imagine that she did.

She closed her eyes and took a deep breath. Apparently she was in no rush to begin the conversation, but unless they started talking he would continue with his inappropriate thoughts. If he walked over and kissed her, would she resist? Or would she part her lips and invite him in?

Finally he had to say something, anything, to keep him from acting on his fantasy. "You picked up that dance step pretty fast."

She opened her eyes and smiled. "Thanks. I should be able to, after fifteen years of ballet and tap."

He liked having another key to her personality. "When was this?"

"My mother enrolled me when I was three. Voice and acting lessons, too, so I'd be a triple threat. She named me after Geena Davis. I was supposed to be a star."

"I didn't know that." Not surprising. What he didn't know about Geena was seriously out of proportion to what he did know. "What happened?"

"A common story." She gave a little shrug. "I can dance and sing okay but I have no talent for acting. If I'd been movie-star beautiful that might have made up for my bad acting, but I'm not."

"I think you look nice." That just popped out. Hadn't meant to say it *at all*.

"Thanks." She smiled and took off her glasses to polish them. "But I would have had to be a real knockout to succeed. Luckily, along the way I discovered that supporting the careers of other actors makes me happy. I've hung out with them all my life, so opening a PR business was a no-brainer. Mom wasn't too pleased with my decision, but she eventually came to grips with it."

"That's good." He sometimes wondered if the woman who'd given birth to him would come out of the woodwork and claim his success was all because of her. "I'll have to admit that I've never seen one of your mother's movies."

"Sad to say, they were forgettable. She blames the scripts and the directing. Personally, I think she's better at creating drama offscreen than on. I was afraid she'd end up with her own reality TV show, but fortunately we were all spared that. She finally gave up trying to draw attention to herself and moved to Italy."

He couldn't get a bead on whether she loved her mother or tolerated her. "Is that a good thing?"

"To be honest, it's a relief. She's exhausting to be around."

"Almost as bad as a day spent trying to get to Sheridan, huh?"

"In retrospect, it wasn't so terrible." She put her glasses back on and pushed away from the railing. "Anyway, I didn't want to go to bed without talking to you about something."

Ah, yes, bedtime. Between the dancing, the beer and finally being alone with her, he was losing the battle with his sexual attraction. She'd be in the bedroom next to his and that would make falling asleep a challenge. When he'd arrived, his mom had asked him if he wanted to bunk in one of the cabins for nostalgia's sake. Knowing he'd be interfering with the cleaning and preparations for the summer school kids, he'd decided not to.

Now he wished he'd opted for the cabin. His mom had obviously accepted Geena, and for all he knew Rosie had put them adjacent to each other on purpose. It would be like her to think it served him right for being so unwelcoming. He wasn't feeling unwelcoming anymore. Life had been so much simpler when he'd thought of Geena as the enemy instead of a sexy woman who might or might not be seeing someone.

She took another deep breath, which strained the buttons on her jacket.

He'd been fascinated by that jacket all evening. It revealed a slight bit of cleavage, and near as he could tell, she wore nothing but a bra or a camisole underneath. She didn't really need a blouse because the jacket provided decent coverage, but he'd thought about what he'd see if he unfastened the buttons.

He needed to get off this train of thought and buy a ticket on another one. Her outfit was no more seductive than any she'd worn in meetings they'd had regarding his career. But those meetings had taken place in her office and not during a cool evening when a silky breeze wafted over them bringing the scent of wild grasses and pine trees.

"You're upset because I invaded your territory." Her voice was soft and weary.

"That did upset me." He wasn't angry now but chose not to say that.

"If I'd only hoped to convince you to go along with my original plan, then coming here would have been obnoxious, but that's not why I booked those flights."

"Then why did you?"

"First of all, I realized that Briana isn't going to let go of this. If you haven't gone online then you might not know, but she's come up with a cutesy slogan and she's plastering it everywhere."

Okay, this topic might effectively cool his jets. "I'm afraid to ask what it is."

"Run, Forrest, run."

"Oh, for God's sake." Just as Geena had predicted, he'd been branded a coward. "That's sickening."

"I agree, but the plain truth is that you're not going to be able to ride this one out. She's portraying your silence and your absence as an admission of guilt and she's spinning stories about how you lusted after her during the filming of *Preston's Revenge*."

His stomach pitched. "That's a damned lie." So much for the seductive ambiance of the porch.

"I know it is."

"How?" Their discussion in her office came back to him along with the anger he'd felt at being wrongly accused. "You weren't there."

"No, but I—"

"Geena, you've always been a straight shooter before. Please don't twist yourself into a pretzel because you like my family and you want to smooth things over."

Her chin lifted and she met his gaze. "That is *not* the case and I resent your implication."

"And I'm suspicious of your sudden turnaround! How can you be so sure I'm telling the truth?" He took a step closer. "Maybe I spent every available moment on location trying to seduce her while she valiantly fought me off."

A flame burned in her eyes, which were definitely green, like he'd thought. "I'm trying to apologize, damn it. You didn't try to seduce her and you didn't kiss her outside that café. A gentleman wouldn't do those things. I allowed the photo to convince me of something I should have known wasn't true. But I finally figured it out."

This was turning into an effing roller coaster. "So you've decided I'm a gentleman?"

"I didn't just *decide*. You've demonstrated it from the beginning with your *yes, ma'am* behavior and your respect for everyone in my office, including the cleaning lady. She made a point of telling me that you showed up late one afternoon after we'd all left and you offered to carry out the trash."

"Who wouldn't?"

"Most people, Matt. So obviously you didn't initiate that embarrassing scene in Burbank and you didn't hit on her during the filming. It doesn't fit your profile. It's not you."

"God, that makes me happy. You can't imagine how happy." Vindicated. Damn, that felt good.

"Because I hadn't put that together, I insulted your sense of honor. No wonder you stomped out of my office. I'm surprised you didn't end our business relationship."

He smiled. "That was my original goal when I thought I'd be escorting you back to town. First I'd get you a hotel room and then I'd fire you."

"Good thing Rosie asked me to stay, huh?"

"I wasn't in favor of that, either."

"Yeah, she robbed you of your chance to fire me." She gazed at him with an expression that bordered on tenderness. "You can still do that if you want, although Rosie seems to think you need me."

The warmth in her eyes brought him right back to the thoughts he'd been having until the discussion turned ugly. Drawn by that warmth, he drifted closer, within touching distance. "I probably do need you. I have no idea how to deal with this fiasco. Anyway, I can't fire you with Rosie around. She'd give me hell for it. The others wouldn't like it, either. You made some friends in there."

"Nice to know." For some reason her glasses misted up. She took them off. "How about out here?"

He was a goner. "I've always liked you. That's why it bothered me so much that you believed I'd caused that scene."

"I've always liked you, too." She moistened her lips. "That's all the more reason I should have stopped to think before I jumped to conclusions."

The gesture caught his attention and he noticed her lipstick had worn off. He'd never seen her without it. Because of that, the natural pink of her bare lips was more arousing than if she'd stripped naked. The sweep of her tongue had left her mouth with a satin sheen that begged to be savored.

"Rosie thinks there's more to it."

"More to what?" While he'd been imagining how she'd taste, he'd lost track of the conversation. Lifting his gaze, he saw awareness in her expression and his heart pounded in anticipation. She knew what he wanted. Judging from the way she was looking at him, she wasn't opposed.

"The kissing incident." Her breathing quickened. "She doesn't think we have all the facts and you won't make those public because you're too much of a gentleman. I'm inclined to agree. There are lines you won't cross."

He searched her expression. "Apparently you admire that."

"I do."

"Then maybe we should head inside."

She swallowed. "We should?"

"Uh-huh. I'm guessing you already have someone in your life."

"Actually, I don't." Her voice was laced with tension. "Why do you want that information?"

"Because I'm two seconds away from kissing you and I'd hate to ruin my sterling reputation."

Color bloomed in her cheeks. "I promise your reputation's safe with me."

Chapter Five

Being kissed by Matt Forrest was the last thing in the world Geena had expected to happen to her in Wyoming. Being trampled by a moose had seemed far more likely, or being eaten by a grizzly bear.

But kicking off her shoes to learn Cade's new dance step had felt like kicking off the traces. She'd been under strain, too, and dancing plus a bottle of beer had relaxed her. She'd forgotten to be so darned professional, and like any good actor, Matt had taken his cue.

Licking her lips had been an innocent and unplanned move, but when those electric-blue eyes had focused on her mouth, game over. A powerful wave of lust had swept her brain clean of everything but the need to kiss and be kissed by the hottest cowboy she'd ever known.

He took off his hat and laid it on a chair. Then he reached for her. Cupping her face in both hands, he gazed into her eyes. "I've thought about doing this for months. How about you?"

She was so excited she could barely breathe. "Never crossed my mind." Sliding her hands up the soft cotton of his T-shirt, she felt the solid muscles underneath. The tactile thrill was more delicious than she could have possibly imagined.

"You're not attracted to me? I could have sworn—"

"I didn't say that." She rubbed her hands across his chest because she couldn't help herself.

"So you are attracted to me."

"Uh-huh." She began a slow massage and watched his eyes darken to navy.

"I should've asked you out. I almost did."

"What stopped you?"

His gaze searched hers. "I thought it might be unprofessional."

"And people talk."

"Tell me about it." He tipped her head back. "But tonight, after watching you dance, I don't really care."

"I don't much care, either." Her pulse raced as she anticipated the touch of his mouth. It looked sexy on screen but ten times more kissable in real life.

He leaned closer. "Glad to hear it." And he captured her mouth.

When he did, the takeover was complete. She leaned into him and ran up the white flag without firing a single shot. No doubt the guy had many talents or he wouldn't be finding success in the competitive film industry. But he could give a master course in the art of mouth-to-mouth contact.

He made the connection effortlessly, as if he'd already mapped the contours of her lips. And once he settled in, heaven help her. The movements of his mouth and tongue were subtle yet devastating. He teased, he sucked and he nibbled until she was ready to rip her clothes off because she wanted his brand of intense pleasure *everywhere*.

That tortured moan had come from her. Her panties were damp and she was clinging to him for dear life. Dimly she remembered they were on the porch of his parents' house and nothing she longed for could happen here.

Gasping in reaction, she struggled out of his arms and backed away. "You should have a license for that mouth."

His chuckle was low and sexy, although he was breathing hard, too. "You were giving as good as you got, lady."

"Okay, Forrest, the gloves are off. We're officially hot for each other."

"I noticed." He dragged in air. "I'm quick that way."

She pressed a hand against her thumping heart. "I'm... I don't know what's supposed to happen next. This is still highly unprofessional."

"Like I said, I don't care anymore."

"Honestly, neither do I. But I'm a guest in your parents' home. I'm not planning to embarrass either me or them."

"We won't." He retrieved his hat and settled it on his head. "But this isn't over."

"I hope not, but I'm a stranger in a strange land. I need a guide."

"Right." He paused. "The first thing you should know is that Mom put you in the room next to mine."

"Oh, geez."

"That might have been an accident but it might not. She could have done it because she was upset with me for being a jerk when you arrived. But I also feel obliged to warn you that when it comes to her boys, she's a matchmaker."

Geena gulped. "But she barely knows me."

"And that may not figure into her thinking at all, but

I might have mentioned you a few times on the phone. That could be enough to set her in motion."

"Oh." Knowing he'd talked to Rosie about her was flattering but she wasn't crazy about being the target of a matchmaking scheme, even if the proposed match was between her and Mr. Hotter than-a-jalapeño.

"I'm really not sure what she's thinking. But she knows that you want the best for me, which is a big deal for her. I'm sure she appreciates your interest in the academy, too. You've made a good first impression."

"I'm glad, but let me be clear. After that dynamite kiss I'm eager to get even friendlier, but it's way too early to be picking out china patterns. Considering my background, I'm not sure that will ever be in the cards."

"I'll call your background and raise you mine. Not to mention the lousy odds of any Hollywood couple lasting more than a few years."

She grimaced. "Isn't that the truth? But it's good that we're on the same page, even if your foster mom has other ideas."

"You know, I shouldn't assume she wants to marry me off just because she has that reputation with her boys. She knows how important my career is, how much I want to make it as an actor. So forget what I said. For sure she wants us to get along for our mutual benefit, but that might be the extent of it."

"Even though she put us in adjoining rooms?"

"Yeah, she did." He shrugged. "I'm not sure what she had in mind when she did that, but in any case, it won't work for me. I'll take a bedroll down to the barn."

"Is that a veiled invitation to join you there?"

"No, ma'am, it isn't."

"Getting it on in the barn has a certain ring to it."

"Been there, but with country girls. I'm not subjecting you to that."

She looked him in the eye. "What if I want to be subjected to it?"

His reaction was all she could have hoped for. His eyes darkened and his chest heaved. But he didn't give in. "Maybe before you leave, but not the first time. For all you know you're allergic to hay. Or horses. Hear me out on this and don't get crazy on me."

"I'm already crazy, and it's your fault because you kiss like no man I've ever known."

"So I've been told."

She groaned. "You could have warned me! I wasn't the least bit prepared!"

"Oh, Geena." Moving closer, he pulled her into his arms. "We've started this thing between us and I promise we'll finish it. I bought a ranch, and I'm thinking that maybe we—"

"A ranch? A whole ranch?"

"I'm hoping it's a whole ranch. I'd hate like hell to buy half a ranch."

That made her laugh. "So, where is it?"

"Right down the road." He rubbed the small of her back. "I vaguely remember the place from when I lived at Thunder Mountain but I've never been inside the house. Rosie and Herb looked it over for me and said it was a good buy, although it needs work. I want to go see it tomorrow, so if you'd like to ride along, you'd be most welcome."

"I'm way ahead of you. I accept your invitation to visit your ranch."

"Excellent."

"Now, let me go or I'm liable to drag you into my SUV and drive you over there tonight."

He backed away. "You're good for my ego."

"You ain't seen nothin' yet."

His gaze swept over her. "We need to get back inside before I change my mind about the barn."

"I'm not allergic to hay. Or horses. I just remembered that I've been exposed to both at Disneyland. I'm good with goats, too." His laughter made her smile. "Well, I am. They came right up to me wagging their little tails."

"I'll bet they did. But please don't come down to the barn tonight. It's not an appropriate venue for what I have in mind, and anyway, I didn't anticipate this so I don't have supplies."

Supplies. He really was a gentleman. "Okay. I'll respect your wishes." She put on her glasses and tucked a few strands of hair back into place.

"Besides, you should get a good night's sleep after what you've been through today."

"What about you, bedding down in the barn? Surely you won't get a good night's sleep."

"Actually, I will. I love listening to the horses moving around in their stalls, munching on hay, making snuffling sounds. It's comforting. I used to do it all the time when I lived here. I'd pretend I was John Wayne, banished to the barn by Maureen O'Hara." He took a deep breath. "Ready to go in?"

"Do I have a choice?" Now she wished that nature had given her red hair so she could be Maureen O'Hara to his John Wayne.

He shook his head. "We've already been out here long enough to raise suspicion. And you must be exhausted."

"I used to be." She glanced at him. "But thanks to you, I'm all revved up again."

"Sorry about that."

"Are you really?"

He grinned. "No, ma'am."

"I didn't think so. When I first arrived and saw your face, I thought I'd made a terrible mistake by coming here. But it wasn't a mistake, was it?"

He met her gaze and his eyes crinkled with laughter. "If it was, I hope you keep on makin' 'em."

Dear Lord, his kiss had been enough to seduce her without adding country charm to the mix. Apparently being in this setting highlighted all his considerable attributes. She could hardly wait for tomorrow's trip to his ranch so she could sample every one of them.

The woman was hotter than the griddle at a Chamber of Commerce pancake breakfast. Matt was forced to call on his acting skills in order to appear in control as he walked back into the living room with Geena. He was congratulating himself on his smooth entrance when he tripped over a footstool and barely saved himself from a face-plant.

"I saw that!" Cade smirked at him. "It was totally the stool's fault."

His face heated. "I was...uh..."

"Distracted?" Lexi gave him an innocent smile.

"Poor guy's worried about Briana." Geena's color was high and she avoided looking at him.

"That's the truth." He appreciated her attempt to excuse his clumsiness but he could tell the rest of them weren't buying it. Even his dad, usually the last to catch on, wore a knowing expression.

His mom stood. "Briana's lucky I don't live in her town. Miserable woman." She turned to Geena. "I'm sure you're ready to crash. Let me show you where everything is. Your bathroom's down the hall and the shower has some idiosyncrasies you'll need to know about."

"I appreciate that, because I would love to take a shower before I go to bed."

Great. Now he'd picture her naked in the shower in the bathroom they'd be sharing during this visit.

"I'm going to turn in, myself," his dad said. "See everybody in the morning."

Once all three had left, Matt sank down on the sofa and blew out a breath.

Cade pushed back his hat and gazed at him. "I don't know if it was good or bad, but whatever happened out there sure has you going, bro."

"It was obviously significant," Lexi said. "You're one of the most coordinated guys I know. You took fencing lessons, for God's sake. You don't trip over footstools."

Matt rubbed the back of his neck. "I kissed her."

Cade nodded as if he'd expected to hear that. "Judging from the glazed look in your eyes, she kissed you back."

"Yes."

"Ah." Lexi chuckled. "What a wealth of information is contained in that one little word. So is it okay for the rest of us to like her, now that you're kissing each other? Because we all pretty much do."

"Yeah, sure." He had trouble collecting his thoughts when his brain had been hijacked. "Do you think Mom's matchmaking?"

"Good question." Cade scratched his chin where the shadow of a beard was starting to show. "Normally I would say yes, but I don't get that vibe from her. We talked about Geena while you two were out there smooching, but—"

"It was *one* kiss."

"Then it must have been a dandy." Cade studied him. "I'm happy for you."

"Me, too," Lexi said. "Earlier tonight, before she

showed up, I got the impression from the conversation that you haven't been dating anyone in the past six months or so."

"I haven't. After auditioning for every commercial in the world, it seemed, I was finally in demand, which was great but kept me really busy. Then this bonanza hit, but a role like that takes a hell of a lot of prep work."

"I'll bet." Compassion shone in her eyes. "You looked strung out when you arrived, but you're a lot perkier after stealing a kiss from your PR rep."

"As well you should be," Cade said. "Geena's great. I regret the nasty things I said about her before."

"But you don't think Mom's up to her usual tricks?"

"I don't think so." Cade turned toward Lexi. "Do you?"

"Why do I get the feeling you three are talking about me?" Rosie walked into the living room looking more amused than upset.

"Guilty." Lexi spoke up immediately. "We were wondering if you were matchmaking between Geena and Matt."

"I'm not." Rosie claimed her favorite chair before gazing at him. "I came out to tell you that I moved her to the room down by us. That way she can have her own bathroom." She paused. "And you won't be neighbors."

He was very likely blushing. "Okay." He calculated whether the added distance would help him sleep any better. Probably not.

"Should've done that in the first place, but I was feeling a little put out with you, so I thought it would serve you right to have her next door. I figured sharing a bathroom might force you to be more civil."

Cade snorted. "I don't think that'll be a problem anymore."

"I can see that." She smiled at Matt. "I don't want to torture you, son. Or her, either. She confessed the strong attraction between you two but said she would never take advantage of my hospitality."

"She said that, straight out?" He gaped at her.

"You sound surprised," Lexi said. "Don't you know people tell Rosie everything? I've never met anyone who inspires people to spill their guts the way Rosie does. It's a gift."

"They don't tell me *everything*." Rosie surveyed the group. "For example, nobody has bothered to mention why Briana Danvers orchestrated that photo op. It was clearly planned and executed for a reason. Appears to be the work of an angry woman, if you ask me." She speared Matt with a look. "I'm sure you have noble intentions, but she doesn't deserve considerate treatment after the way she's behaved."

"That's what I said when he—" Cade groaned. "Sorry, Matt."

Rosie nodded as she studied the two of them. "As I suspected, it all came out on the drive from the airport." She turned her attention to Matt. "Well?"

He shook his head. "Sorry, Mom."

"You don't trust me to keep it to myself?"

"Of course I do." He sent a pleading glance in Cade's direction, but Cade only spread his hands in bewilderment.

"Maybe you don't trust *me*," Lexi said.

"I'd trust both of you with my life. Trust isn't the issue."

Rosie leaned forward. "Then what is the issue? I want to help you get out of this mess but I feel handicapped because I don't know the whole story. I assume Geena doesn't know it, either."

"No, she doesn't."

"She probably should. It might be extremely important."

"I can't tell you what happened unless you promise that you won't take any action against Briana."

"Action?" Rosie blinked. "What kind of action would I take?"

"I don't know, but you both have to promise not to try and harm her by word or deed."

"Wow," Lexi said. "This is getting intense. Want us to sign something in blood?"

Matt sighed. "Your word is good enough."

"All right," Rosie said. "Lexi and I promise not to harm that horrible woman." She paused. "Or hire someone to do it for us."

Cade choked on his beer.

Rosie waited until he'd settled down before turning back to Matt. "What happened?"

As Matt described Briana's behavior, his mom grew very still, but her fists clenched and her eyes glittered with an unholy fire.

He finished the story and took a deep breath. "It's safe to say she's after revenge."

Rosie looked at him and her voice sounded deceptively calm. "I could strangle her with my bare hands." The even tone coupled with the ring of certainty was a chilling combination. She didn't get angry often, but when she did everyone knew to take a step back.

He cleared his throat. "Mom, you promised not to—"

"And I won't. She's not worth going to jail for. I wouldn't dirty my hands on that piece of trash. But poor Cliff."

"He's the one I'm protecting, not her."

"Just realize you won't be able to protect him forever.

I doubt you're the first and you won't be the last. He'll find out sooner or later. Probably sooner now that everyone and his dog is online."

"But Matt doesn't want to be the bearer of bad news," Lexi said. "I get that. Cliff Wallace seems like a great guy."

"From what I've read about him, he is." Rosie leaned back in her chair. "But I think he has a weakness for bad women. I should have known this one would be no different. She won't last, but in the meantime, she's caused problems for one of my own." She glanced at Matt. "There must be some way to put a hitch in her giddyup."

"Don't I wish," he said, "but I'm fresh out of ideas."

"We're all too tired to think about this now." His mom stood. "We'll tackle it tomorrow. But thanks for trusting me with the info."

"It wasn't about trust." He got up to give her a good-night hug. "Cade and I were worried the mama grizzly might fly to LA and do a number on Briana."

"And wouldn't I love to! But I won't." She hugged him back. Then she said good-night to Cade and Lexi before walking back down the hallway.

"I think that went okay," Cade said after she left. "Sorry I slipped up, though."

"No worries." Matt continued to gaze at the darkened hallway as he debated whether his mom's room-juggling trick changed anything. "Once we got into the conversation about Briana, I knew she'd find a way to dig it out of me."

"Like Lexi said, it's her gift." Cade stood and came over to sling an arm around Matt's shoulders. "I notice how you're focused on that hallway and who's sleeping at the end of it."

"Just thinking."

"I know how that goes. I don't want to get all up in your business, but—"

"Yeah, you do." Matt turned to smile at him.

"Let's just say that Mom's maneuver with the room switcheroo is well meant, but I doubt it'll lower your stress level. I suggest an alternate plan. Lexi and I have a comfy sofa you can use tonight. That should keep you out of trouble for the time being."

"And we'd be glad to have you as our guest," Lexi added.

"Thanks, but I think I'll just head down to the barn and make up a bedroll in an empty stall."

Cade nodded. "That works, too. I remember you used to like doing that, getting into your John Wayne persona."

Matt lowered his voice and moved closer to Cade. "Buddy, this is awkward as hell, but I have a problem if things heat up in the next day or two. I don't have—"

"Say no more," Cade murmured.

His color high, Matt glanced over at Lexi. "Don't listen."

"Can't hear a thing."

"Got you covered," Cade said quietly.

"Thanks."

"All righty, then." Cade clapped him on the back. "We'll shove off. See you in the—well, hello, sunshine."

Matt glanced toward the hallway.

Geena stood there rubbing her eyes. Her glossy brown hair tumbled in waves over her shoulders and she wore a bright blue sleep shirt with a Captain America shield on the front. She put on her glasses and peered at them. "Why is everybody still up? I thought we had to be awake at dawn."

"We're in the process of leaving," Cade said. "Why are you up?"

Matt was grateful for Cade's response because he was incapable of making one. His tongue was stuck to the roof of his mouth as he noticed the drape of her sleep shirt and concluded she wasn't wearing a bra. That could mean she didn't have on panties, either. The ends of her hair were still damp from the shower.

"I was thirsty and needed a glass for water."

Lexi started for the kitchen. "I'll get you one. There's a pitcher of cold water in the fridge. You'd probably rather have that."

"Thanks, I would. I'll come with you. I need to know where things are." Her bare feet whispered over the hardwood floor as she followed Lexi.

Matt gazed after her, still at a loss for words. She was supposed to be tucked in her room with the door closed, not out here roaming around in a Captain America sleep shirt with nothing underneath but warm, sensuous, freshly showered woman.

"You poor slob." Cade regarded him with sympathy. "There's no way I could slip you those raincoats tonight. Want us to hang around for a few, make sure she goes back to her designated area?"

"That's okay. I can handle it."

"Yeah, that's what I'm afraid of."

Chapter Six

The hum of conversation in the living room had traveled through the air ducts to Geena's room. She hadn't been able to make out any of it, which had been maddening. For sure she was missing something and it might be important.

She'd been dying to know what they were talking about, specifically what Matt was talking about. What if he'd decided to reveal the backstory that had led to Briana's stunt? Damn it, now she wasn't the least bit sleepy.

She mostly blamed Matt's kiss, although to be fair she was still on California time and she never went to bed this early. But it was after eleven here and people were still in the living room talking, even though Rosie had said they generally weren't night owls. That meant something special was going on and she wanted to know what it was.

When she couldn't stand it another minute, she'd come up with an excuse to go out there. She would have put on a robe, but she'd packed so quickly this morning that she hadn't thought to bring one. The sleep shirt was cotton, opaque and reached to midthigh. It covered everything important and she didn't consider it seductive.

At least, she hadn't until she'd noticed Matt's expression once she put on her glasses. He'd looked as if someone had blinded him with a strobe light.

Sadly, she seemed to have caught the tail end of the party. After Lexi poured her a glass of water from the fridge, the two of them walked back to the living room. Geena had hoped that everyone would sit down and continue the discussion, but although Cade seemed ready to stay, Lexi insisted on leaving.

After they were gone Geena was alone with Matt. She realized that might not be the best combination, considering how Matt was looking at her. She should take her water and go, but she wanted to know what that conversation had been about and she believed in seizing the moment. "Part of the reason I couldn't sleep is that I heard you guys talking out here."

That startled him. "You did?"

"Through the air ducts. But I couldn't understand what you were saying."

"Oh. Yeah, I forgot about the air duct thing. Sorry if we kept you awake." He didn't look particularly sorry. The gleam in his eyes returned.

"If it's private family stuff, then never mind."

"It kind of was." His expression said clearly that he'd like to drop the subject and move on to other things, like maybe kissing.

She wouldn't object, but she had a point to make first. "Matt, if you were giving them the scoop on your history with Briana, then I deserve to hear it, too. We're in this together."

"Nice to know." He took a step closer and there was no mistaking the intent in those blue eyes.

The huskiness in his voice fired her blood and fogged her glasses, but she recognized a delaying tactic when she saw one. "As long as we're working together, your reputation is connected with mine." She took off her glasses and used her shirtsleeve to clean them. "If I let you go down in flames that won't look good for my firm. I don't want to make this all about me because my investment in the problem isn't nearly as big as yours. But I do have a stake in it."

"I hadn't thought of that." Taking off his hat, he ran his fingers through his hair.

After yesterday, she recognized the gesture as a sign of nervousness. He didn't like talking about this and he'd already been through it once tonight. "I'm sorry if this is difficult, but I need to know."

"I understand, but the more people I tell, the more likely it'll come out and I don't want that."

"You're my client. I won't betray your confidence."

He studied her for a moment and a smile tugged at the corners of his mouth.

"What?"

"Can't doubt the sincerity of someone wearing a Captain America shirt." He used his hat to motion her toward the sofa. "We might as well sit."

She took one end and he claimed the other, leaving at least three feet between them. It wasn't enough. She could feel the air crackling in that empty space every time she looked into his eyes.

He laid his hat, brim side up, between them.

She glanced at it. "Is that the neutral zone?"

"Yes, ma'am." His wink gave her goose bumps.

"I promise not to attack you."

"I can't make that promise." His gaze swept over her. "Not when you come out here looking like that."

"Sorry. I forgot to bring a robe."

"I'm not complaining, just stating the facts." His attention settled on the Captain America shield again. "I take it you're a fan?"

"Sure. He's an all-American good guy. Like you."

"Thanks for the reminder. It'll help me stay on my side of the hat." He pointed to the glass she held. "You're not drinking your water."

"The water was an excuse to come out here to see what was going on."

He sighed. "All right. Let's get this over with." Glancing away, he cleared his throat. "You probably won't be surprised to hear that Briana propositioned me."

She sucked in a breath.

"So you are surprised."

"I shouldn't be, but *damn her*." The news made her sick to her stomach. The woman was a predator if she'd take advantage of a guy who'd just gotten his first big break.

"I'd hoped she was kidding around, but when I tried to make a joke out of it she set me straight real fast."

Geena's stomach churned. "That explains everything. You know what they say. *Hell hath no fury like a woman scorned.*"

"I did *not* scorn her." He tunneled his fingers through his hair again and swore. "God knows I wanted to. I was furious, but I was also humiliated. I wanted her to like and respect me for my acting, but you know what? I wonder if she was jealous of the attention I got. Maybe she thought that if we had sex she'd have some leverage, some power over me." He glanced over. "Does that make sense?"

"Unfortunately it makes perfect sense." Her heart ached for the loss of his idealistic dreams. Briana had ruined what should have been special.

"I knew that yelling would make things worse so I tried to be nice. I had to think of something that didn't sound insulting, so I made up a personal rule—never get involved with a costar. I don't have any damned rule like that. It sounds stupid and anal, especially coming from somebody as green as I am, but I tried to make it sound believable."

"But you still rejected her."

"I had to! But I swear I wasn't mean about it."

"Doesn't matter. Once she made a move, she put you in a no-win situation."

"Are you saying I can't win this fight?"

"No, I'm definitely not saying that." She considered telling him that he had all the ammunition he needed right here on this ranch—his background as a foster kid, his bond with his foster brothers, his amazing foster parents and his scholarship plan to support the new venture. All he had to do was turn her loose on this PR bonanza and everyone would forget about the stupid scandal as they soaked up Matt's touching past.

But she could predict his response to that idea, especially after a long and emotional day. Timing was everything. "We'll figure this out, and I'm grateful to you for taking me into your confidence. Obviously it's a painful episode and we don't have to bring it up again." She stood.

He got to his feet, too. "You can see why I don't want this to come out, right?"

"Yes, I do. Besides, it would be tacky and pointless to accuse her of trying to seduce you. That could really backfire on us."

"And it would hurt Cliff."

She sighed. "You're gonna have to let that one go. He married a toxic woman. That decision will come back to bite him eventually, and everyone who knows and loves him will hate seeing it happen. But it can't be helped."

"Rosie said basically the same thing." He scrubbed a hand over his face. "He was in Utah with us for a couple of weeks. He was great, always complimenting me on my work and encouraging me whenever I struggled with a scene."

"I'll bet Briana hated that. I'm guessing his primary job is telling her *she's* fabulous. No wonder she propositioned you. She could gain power over you and punish her husband at the same time."

"Guess so." He looked destroyed. "And now, if he believes Briana's lies, which he has to since he loves her, he must hate my guts."

She closed the gap between them. "Matt, I'm so sorry. We'll fix it."

"I hope so." His troubled gaze searched hers. "I'm glad you're here."

"Me, too." She reached up and stroked his cheek. "It'll be okay. I promise."

He muttered an oath and drew her close. "I shouldn't be doing this. But God, you smell good."

"I shouldn't be doing this, either." She slid her arms around his waist and nestled against him. Sure enough, her glasses misted and she couldn't see him. "Wait. I need to take off—"

"*Don't.* Once I see you naked I won't be able to stop."

"I meant my glasses." She pulled them off and held them in her hand.

"Oh. I could work around those."

"But they fog up whenever we...whenever I..."

"I'm not surprised." His gaze roamed her face. "We generate a hell of a lot of heat." He shuddered. "I need you, Geena. One kiss. Just one." And his lips came down on hers.

She held tight as his big body trembled with the force of his powerful emotions and his attempt to keep them in check.

His tongue thrust deep as he lifted her hips to meet the hard ridge of his erection. He pressed forward with an urgency that tightened her core as moisture gathered between her thighs. She whimpered, yearning for that connection that he promised with each stroke of his tongue but ultimately would deny her, at least for tonight.

And then, as if a storm had passed, he gently eased away. Keeping his hands at her waist to steady her, he raised his head and gulped for air. "Enough."

Breathing hard, she looked into eyes that glittered with passion. "Is it?"

"For now." He paused and took a breath. "It has to be." He let go of her and stepped back. "I shouldn't have started that. But I…it helps when I can hold you."

"I'm glad."

"But this isn't the place or the time. I'm going to the barn."

"Me, too."

Smiling faintly, he glanced down at her bare feet. "I think not."

"You can carry me." She felt safe saying that because of all his lovely muscles.

"Lady, you are temptation personified." He swallowed. "But I want you to stay here." He reached out and stroked her cheek with the tip of his finger. "Please. I'd rather not take a chance that we'd get so involved that a member of my family would find us in the morning, all tangled up together and naked as the day we were born."

"I guess you've had enough embarrassment for a while, huh?"

"Actually, I was thinking of your embarrassment."

A surge of warmth moved through her, warmth that had little to do with sex. "Thank you, Matt."

"Don't give me too much credit. I was this close to pulling off your sleep shirt a moment ago, despite what I said."

"But you didn't."

"You whimpered as if I was being too rough. That was enough to bring me to my senses."

"For future reference, I wasn't whimpering because you were being too rough."

"You weren't?"

"When I make that little noise it means I'm frustrated beyond belief and I'm hoping you'll take care of the issue immediately."

"Oh."

"Just FYI."

He picked up his hat and settled it on his head. "Probably a good thing I didn't know that." He touched the tips of his fingers to the brim. "See you in the mornin'." And he walked out the front door.

Geena's questions had been answered by the interlude with Matt, even if her libido hadn't been satisfied. Apparently answers were more important than orgasms right now because she slept soundly until her phone chimed at five in the morning. Dawn would break in fifteen minutes.

Obviously the birds outside her window hadn't gotten the memo. They chirped and chattered as if the sun had come up an hour ago. Must be the early birds determined to get that worm. Which was a gross image, now that she thought about it.

Ten minutes later, her hair in a ponytail and wearing a tiny bit of makeup because she'd be seeing Matt, she put on a pair of beige linen pants and a green silk blouse. Until Rosie coughed up some cowgirl duds, it was the best she could do. Her open-toed slides didn't seem appropriate, either, but at least she wouldn't go prancing down to the barn in four-inch heels.

As she walked through the living room she heard Rosie rattling pans in the kitchen, but she didn't stop to chat. She'd promised to be down at the barn by five fifteen and she would, by golly, honor that promise. Anticipation curled in her stomach the way it used to on Christmas morning when she was little. Those mornings might be the only times she'd been up at dawn.

Despite her mother's many failings as a parent, she'd always made a big deal about Christmas. She and her boyfriend du jour would be standing at the foot of the stairs, their arms loaded with gifts. Another big pile would be waiting under the tree.

On some level, Geena had known the truckload of presents stemmed from her mother's guilt because the rest of the year she'd left Geena in the care of Beatrice, the nanny. Beatrice had always spent Christmas with her family, so the holiday had been all on Geena's mom. When it came to extravagance, her mother had written the book.

But as Geena stepped out on the front porch, the commercial splendor of her childhood seemed tawdry compared to the scene spread before her. The ground sparkled as if diamonds had been scattered there, and she finally realized it was dew touched by sunlight. And, oh, the mountains! She'd driven in after dark and she'd been too worried about getting lost to notice the dim bulk of the range that stretched as far as she could see.

Shadows chased by the rising sun moved gently downward from peaks still tipped with snow. If she lived here she'd never get anything done. She'd spend all her time on the porch in an Adirondack chair watching the light shift on the mountain slopes.

A horse whinnied. She'd left her prescription sunglasses in her room, so she shaded her eyes with her hand as she glanced in the direction of the sound. The barn doors slid open with a soft rumble and Matt walked out to gaze up at the house. He was looking for her!

Her pulse raced at the sight of him framed in the doorway of the barn. He had on a white T-shirt, possibly the same one he'd worn the night before. After all, he'd slept down there. She waved and started toward him.

He waited for her, and she found that incredibly sweet. He could have ducked back in to help with the chores, but instead, he'd made welcoming her a priority. Too bad she couldn't get there faster, but her open-toed shoes weren't happy with the uneven terrain. She'd rather not embarrass herself by falling down on her way to the barn.

When she drew close enough, he called out a greeting. "You look great!"

"Not exactly Western wear."

"Doesn't matter." He walked to meet her. "You climbed out of bed and made it down here for feeding time." He hadn't shaved, and his rakish grin made him look like a certified bad boy.

If he had a rebellious streak, he kept it firmly in check. But last night she'd caught an exciting glimpse of his wild side. She liked it.

He wrapped an arm around her shoulders. "I like the ponytail. Sassy."

"Thanks."

"You impress me, Geena Lysander."

"That makes it mutual." If she could wake up to the sight of Matt in a snug T-shirt and jeans every morning, she'd have no problem becoming an early riser. He would inspire any woman to sacrifice a little sleep. "But I don't want to interrupt your work."

"Since I slept down here, I had some of it done before my dad and Cade came. They sent me out to see if you were on your way. And here you are."

"I hope I didn't miss everything."

"Oh, no. I shoveled stalls instead of feeding. I knew you wanted to watch that part. Let's go let them know you're here and then I'll introduce you around."

"But I already know Herb and Cade."

"I meant introduce you to the horses."

"Oh! Then I'd be delighted to meet them. I don't think I've ever been personally introduced to a horse. Like I said yesterday, I have no experience with them."

"Then we should change that. They're amazing animals." Matt paused before heading down the wooden barn aisle. "She's here!"

"Excellent!" Cade poked his head out of one of the stalls.

"Hey, Geena!" Herb walked toward them. "Come on back. I was about to feed Lucy and Linus."

"Then let's start with them," Matt said. "I promised to introduce her to everybody. She's never met a horse face-to-face."

Herb chuckled and reached into his pocket. "Then it's a good thing I brought carrots." He handed her six chunks. "Give them three apiece. Those two love their carrots."

She put the pieces in the pocket of her pants and decided not to worry if they left a stain. She'd have fun explaining it to the dry cleaner.

"I'd start with Lucy," Herb said. "She gets her nose bent out of shape if her son gets treats before she does." He motioned toward the last stall. "That's Lucy."

A golden horse with a white streak down her nose put her head over the stall door and whinnied.

"She's gorgeous!" Geena gazed at the sleek animal. "She looks just like Roy Rogers's horse!"

Matt glanced at her in surprise. "I thought you didn't know horses."

"I don't, but I know movies. My mother has a collection like you wouldn't believe." Then she noticed another horse, nearly identical, peeking out from the neighboring stall. "Two of them! Lucy and Linus. I see the family resemblance."

Herb folded his arms and beamed. "Amazing, isn't it? You don't always get a palomino foal just because you have a palomino mare, let alone one with a blaze that's almost identical. Linus just had his first birthday. He was born here last May."

"Wow." Geena stared at the young horse. "He looks pretty big to me. They must grow fast."

"He's big," Herb said, "but he's not nearly filled out yet. And he's still a kid at heart. You can go ahead and give Lucy her carrots whenever you want."

"Okay." She approached Lucy, who looked extremely interested in the hand she'd shoved in her pocket. "How do I do it?"

"One piece at a time and rest it on your palm." Matt

walked up to stand beside her. "Hold your hand flat, like this." He straightened out her fingers. "Perfect."

He'd only touched her fingers, yet she felt a zing in every cell of her body. "So, I just hold out my hand and she'll take it?"

"Yes, ma'am."

She was growing very fond of his country manners. Shoot, she was growing very fond of him. If they'd been in LA she might not have allowed herself to give in to this attraction, but circumstances had changed. She expected the dynamic to reverse when they went back. Once again he'd be in a goldfish bowl and they'd need to rethink their arrangement.

Then Lucy began to nuzzle her palm in search of the carrot, and she forgot all about what would or wouldn't happen in a week or so. A horse was eating from her hand. It tickled, making her giggle. She pulled out another carrot and repeated the process. "Matt, I love this."

His soft laughter danced along her nerve endings. "Knew you would."

Chapter Seven

Watching Geena feed carrots to Lucy and Linus caused a major shift in Matt's thinking. She wasn't dressed for hanging out in a barn, but despite that, she looked as if she belonged here. He'd figured she'd like the horses and he'd been right about that. Her uninhibited delight as she interacted with them for the first time was touching.

But until this moment he'd thought of her as a city girl getting a taste of country living. She might enjoy the visit, but without any prior experience to draw on she'd be a fish out of water. Not so. She already fit in, even without the right clothes or any knowledge of horse behavior.

Cade wandered down to join the group and then took her over to meet his sleek black gelding, Hematite. The horse had good manners, thanks to Cade's training, but Hematite didn't warm up to everyone. He warmed right up to Geena, though, leaning into her hand as she scratched his neck the way Cade had shown her.

Herb came over to stand next to Matt. "She seems to be having a good time."

"Yep."

"That incident with Briana is unfortunate and I wish it had never happened, but at least it brought us Geena."

"True." *It brought us Geena.* Like she was a gift. He was beginning to think she was.

"I like her, son. She's welcome anytime."

"I'm sure she'll appreciate knowing that." So did he. Over the years, he'd learned to trust his dad's instincts regarding people. His mom was no slouch in that department, either. Many times in the three years he'd lived in LA he'd wished one or both of them had been on hand to size up a situation.

Geena finished loving on Hematite, and she and Cade started back down the barn aisle. "Cade says it's time to turn them out into the pasture but he thinks I should meet Navarre and Isabeau first."

"Absolutely." Matt glanced at his dad. "Do you want to do the honors of introducing them?"

"You go ahead. In fact, if you and Geena could turn out all the horses when you're finished, that would be a big help. Cade and I have to go fiddle with the automatic watering system."

"Cade's going to help you?" Matt wondered if this was a joke. His brother had many talents, but dealing with mechanical malfunctions wasn't one of them.

"I know it sounds crazy," Cade said, "but I've developed a basic understanding of this pain-in-the-ass watering system."

"That said, I'm still planning to replace it." Herb grimaced. "Darn thing is always acting up. If you decide to put one in over at your new place, don't get this brand."

Matt laughed. "Okay. But I'm a long way from installing a watering system in the barn. I haven't bought a horse, yet."

"Just warning you in advance that this outfit manufactures lemons. Come on, Cade, maybe you can jerry-rig that confounded hose one more time." Herb started toward the back of the barn.

"I'm at your service." With a tip of his hat to Matt and Geena, Cade followed Herb.

"You'll have a horse on your ranch?" Geena's eyes lit up.

"At least two." Now that his brother and his dad were at the other end of the barn, he felt more comfortable putting his arm around her as they walked over to Navarre's stall.

"You must be planning to take people out riding. That sounds like fun." Her comment sounded wistful, as if she'd like that.

"You're invited anytime."

"I'll remember that."

"But, to be totally honest, that's not the main reason I'd buy two. Horses get nervous if there's only one of them. They're herd animals." He stopped in front of Navarre's stall and clucked to the dark chestnut. "Hey, boy. Come on over and meet Geena."

"Look at you, Navarre," she crooned. "You're a handsome guy, just like your namesake." She reached out to stroke the nose that Navarre poked over the stall door.

"I take it your mom owned *Ladyhawke*, too."

"She did, but I bought my own copy. I watch it every year or two. Now when I do, I'll think of this beautiful horse."

He hoped she'd think of him, too. No guarantees on that, though. A crisis had thrown them into close contact, but once the crisis was over, who knew what would happen? Maybe she'd fall in love with Wyoming and want to spend more time here with him, and maybe she wouldn't.

He gave her shoulder a squeeze. "Ready to meet Isabeau?"

"Sure. And there she is, right there waiting for us." She moved closer to the stall door. "Hi, Isabeau, sweetheart." She stroked the mare's glossy neck. "You're a dainty girl, aren't you?" She looked up at Matt. "Why aren't they in the same stall?"

"I doubt they'd want that." He tried not to smile because she was adorably serious with that question.

"Navarre and Isabeau don't like each other?"

"They do, but that doesn't mean they want to share a stall. As you can see, that would be close quarters. They enjoy having their own space."

"Were they ever in the same stall?"

"Truthfully, I doubt it. They might not mirror the *Ladyhawke* movie script, but they like each other. I'd go so far as to say they're devoted to each other. They're a good choice to take out for a two-person trail ride. If there's time, maybe we could…oh, wait. Lexi offered to give you a lesson. That's probably a better idea, to start with her. She's an excellent teacher and I want you to have a good experience."

"Are you offering to take me on a trail ride?"

"I was, but then I remembered about Lexi. And I'm sure your time here is limited. When do you fly back?"

"When we've figured out how to deal with Briana."

He stared at her as he processed the meaning of that statement. "You didn't buy a round-trip ticket?"

"Nope. We need a game plan and I don't see the point in flying home without one. I can't predict how long it will take to come up with something, so I didn't buy a return ticket yet."

"That makes no sense. You have other clients. You can't hang out with me in Wyoming and ignore them."

"I won't ignore them. I'll check in with Larissa on a regular basis. She's in charge while I'm gone, but I intend to keep tabs on things by phone and email. She'll let me know if anything major happens."

"I suppose most things can be handled that way."

"Most things." She gazed at him. "But not this issue."

"Because I turned off my phone. I'm surprised you haven't yelled at me for doing that."

"How could I? You turned it off because I wasn't being helpful. Cutting off communication forced me to dig a little deeper and figure out why you didn't want to talk to me. I knew we had to work it out in person, so here I am. The more time we can spend doing that, the sooner I can get back."

Now, there was a challenging puzzle. The more they were together, the less time she'd be here. "So a trail ride with me would suit you?"

"I'd love it, especially if I can take my phone to keep tabs on the office."

"Absolutely."

"You were right about horses being incredible animals. There's no doubt Lexi has a lot to teach me, but I'll bet I could sit on a gentle horse and ride down the trail without falling off."

"I'm sure you could. I want to put in some time cleaning cabins first thing today, but we might be able to pack a lunch and go out around noon."

"I'll help with the cabins. We can brainstorm while we're cleaning."

"Yeah, no." Laughing, he shook his head. "Not happening."

"Why not? Scrubbing and thinking go great together."

"I could be wrong, but I don't think my mom's going to let you muck out cabins. Just a guess."

"I know how to clean. My nanny, Beatrice, used to let me help her. It was fun, although Beatrice made me swear I wouldn't tell my mother."

"I'm sure you're amazing with a mop, but you're a guest."

"Uninvited guest."

"Trust me, nobody thinks of you that way now. You won't be allowed to clean."

She frowned at him. "I didn't come here to sit around like some princess while everyone else works."

"You feel strongly about this."

"Yes, I do. Your family needs us to help, not hinder."

"Then maybe we can work out a compromise with my mom. We'll offer to tackle a few jobs together in the morning, and then as a reward we'll pack a lunch and take off on a trail ride. She might go for that, especially if you tell her you like to clean."

"All right. We'll try that approach."

"Great. Now, let's get these critters out to the pasture."

"Will I get to see them run?"

"Linus will run, for sure. Sometimes he convinces Hematite to play chase with him. But let's start with Navarre and Isabeau. Want to help me lead 'em out?"

"Yes!"

So he fetched a couple of lead ropes from the tack room. She took to the process as if she'd been doing it her whole life. When all the horses had been turned out, he leaned shoulder to shoulder with her at the gate as they watched Linus and Hematite kick up their heels.

She followed their movements, laughing as they bucked and spun, gold and ebony coats gleaming in the sunlight. "So beautiful."

He studied her profile—the high, intelligent forehead, deep-set eyes and determined chin. She'd chosen to wear glasses instead of contacts, and he thought that suited her straightforward personality. Her smile dimpled her cheek and a breeze coaxed strands of her hair out of her ponytail to curl at her nape. "Yes, ma'am," he murmured. "Beautiful."

She glanced over at him, her green eyes filled with happiness. "Flattery will get you everywhere."

"It's not flattery. It's the truth."

"Thank you, Matt. I feel beautiful when you look at me like that. I also want to kiss the living daylights out of you."

"I'd be fine with it if I didn't see my dad and Cade coming out of the barn."

"I thought they might be, which is why I didn't lay one on you." She pushed away from the gate. "Let's go have some of that breakfast Lexi's so keen on. Where is she, by the way? I can't imagine her sleeping in."

Matt took her hand as they walked back to the house. "Cade said she's updating her website. She never seems to find the time, and she's added some new features to her riding clinics."

"Clinics, huh? Obviously there's more to her job description than just *riding teacher*."

"A lot more. She gives clinics all over, even out of the state. Sure you don't want to take a lesson from her before we go on a trail ride?"

"Let's do the trail ride as planned. If she's so busy she doesn't have time for her website, she might have trouble working me in."

"She'll make the time."

"I know she will. She doesn't seem like the type who

reneges on a promise, but a simple trail ride sounds easy enough unless you think I can't handle it."

"You can and it'll be fun." His body warmed with anticipation. She might be focused on discussing their PR problem on that trail ride, but he had some ideas that had nothing to do with business. Cade had brought a box of condoms down to the barn this morning. Matt had hidden it in the tack room behind some old blankets, but not before he'd pocketed a few.

He'd planned to take her over to his ranch, but he didn't know what he'd find there. Last night, desperate for private time, he'd thought a trip to his recently purchased ranch would be perfect. In the light of day he couldn't picture making out in dusty, empty rooms.

A trail ride had all kinds of things going for it, though—fresh air, wildflowers and grassy meadows. If he wanted to do a subtle sales job on Wyoming, a trail ride to a picturesque clearing he knew about and a picnic on a soft blanket should do the trick.

"I don't know how to explain it," she said, "but being around horses feels very natural to me. Maybe that's because of all the movies I watched, although somehow I never imagined that *I* could ride. My life was crammed with lessons aimed at making me a performer. My mom would have considered riding a hobby, like knitting or scrapbooking. I didn't have time for hobbies."

"How about now?"

"What a thought! I've been concentrating on building my business, but why not have some hobbies?" She glanced at him. "Do you have any?"

"Not yet. But I figure my ranch will qualify once I get everything set up."

"Oh, it will. I imagine it as a place to de-stress and get back to basics."

"That's exactly my vision. You just nailed it."

"Matt, I have the best idea."

"What?"

"Your ranch is nearby, right?"

"Yes, ma'am. I wanted to be close to my folks."

"That's perfect, then! We can ride to your ranch and have lunch there. Your first meal in your new home. Can we do that? I really want to see it."

"Uh, okay, but I don't know what shape the place will be in. The house is empty of furniture, far as I know, and I'll bet there's dust an inch thick on—"

"I don't care about that. We can open the windows to let in fresh air. I'll bet Rosie has a dustpan and whisk-broom we could take along. We'll clear a spot and spread a blanket on the floor. I would be so honored to be the first person you entertain at your ranch."

"And I'd be honored to have you." So much for his picnic in the meadow, but maybe this would be better.

"I think everyone needs a place to get away from the pressures of a job, but judging from my experience, actors may need it more than most."

"I wouldn't have thought so, but now I do."

"Do you regret getting into the business?"

"Never. I had some bad moments after the story broke, but it's my life. I love what I do."

"I've never asked why you chose this kind of work."

They'd reached the steps and he paused to glance at her. "No, you haven't."

"Is it the wrong question to ask? I can withdraw it."

He could smell bacon and coffee. He was hungry and wanted nothing more than to head on inside to enjoy the breakfast Rosie had prepared. But he and Geena were making a connection, and this would come up eventually.

"No, don't withdraw it." He held her gaze. "Just know that none of this can ever go in a press release."

"I would never repeat something you told me without your permission."

"Then I'll make it short, and then we won't have to talk about that anymore, either."

"Okay."

He took a deep breath. He hadn't told this story in a while. None of his new friends in LA had a clue he was a foster kid. "I never knew who my dad was and my mom didn't enjoy having me around."

Her green eyes clouded. "That's hard to imagine."

"Don't worry. Rosie got me counseling and I've accepted that it wasn't my fault. I was in the way of her delusional plan that a guy would come along and sweep her off her feet. Maybe it happened. One day she was supposed to pick me up from school and she never showed."

"Oh, Matt."

"I finally got a friend's mom to give me a ride home and I found a note that said she'd gone to look for a better life. She left the phone number for the foster care division of the town's social services and I called it. Rosie was still working in that department then, and she offered to take me. End of story."

Geena swallowed. "Have you ever heard from your mother?"

"No, ma'am, and I'd rather not." He tugged the brim of his hat lower. "At this point, by her standards, I'm rich and she might think she could cash in."

"I'd like to see her try!"

Geena's protectiveness made him smile. It also made him glad he'd told her. "Thanks for that."

"Maybe you should give me her name in case she has the nerve to contact you through me."

"Mindy's her first name, but no telling what her last name is now. It could have changed six times since then."

"If anybody named Mindy comes looking for you, I'll let you know." She gazed at him. "And I had the audacity to whine about my childhood."

"Money doesn't make everything okay. You had it tough, too. Don't forget that I ended up with Rosie and Herb, plus all my brothers. The way I look at it, my birth mom did me a favor. She went looking for a better life, and thanks to her *I* found one."

"I suppose, in a way, she did the right thing. She wasn't a positive influence."

"Except she was the reason I got into acting. Whenever the school put on a play, I was the first to stick my hand in the air. It was my favorite escape, a chance to pretend I was someone else."

"But when you came here, you didn't give it up. That much I do know about you from your résumé. You were in a ton of high school productions."

"By then I was hooked. If I could make an audience laugh or cry, or even get mad, I was thrilled. Now I'll have to go to my own movies to get that buzz."

"Or take a shot at live theater."

"Maybe."

She stood on tiptoe and brushed a kiss over his cheek. "Thank you for trusting me with your story. It won't go anywhere."

Pushing back his hat, he took her by the shoulders and gave her a quick, fiery kiss. Then he noticed that her glasses were fogged and began to laugh. "I see what you mean about steaming things up. Let me help." He gently took them off and pulled a bandanna out of his back pocket. "I hope I end up doing this a lot." He cleaned the lenses and carefully slid the glasses back into place. "In fact, I'd kiss you again right now, but it's almost time for breakfast."

"Can I have a rain check?"

"Lady, you can have anything you want from me."

Chapter Eight

She could have anything she wanted from Matt. Geena wished she believed it, but she knew his comment didn't extend to whatever she had in mind for his goodwill campaign. He'd made it clear that his foster-kid story was off the table. Now that he'd told her the details, she understood why.

As she tucked into what was possibly the best breakfast she'd ever eaten, she reviewed the situation. Before hearing that his mother had abandoned him, she'd hoped he'd consent to a heartwarming article or video interview about how Rosie, Herb, his foster brothers and this ranch had shaped his life. She'd discovered that trying to refute bad publicity never worked, but replacing it with good news almost always did.

Unfortunately, she couldn't use the Thunder Mountain angle. Once she opened that door, celebrity gossip magazines would dig for the story behind the story. An enterprising reporter might find his mother. Or his mother would contact him. Since he didn't want that, they'd have to take a different approach.

She had no idea what that would be, but the conversation at the breakfast table had shifted from the weather to what everyone planned to do after breakfast. That was her cue to propose the cleaning plan. She glanced across at Matt, who gave her a subtle nod.

Somehow, in the midst of taking seats at the round table, they'd ended up on opposite sides. Herb and Rosie sat on her right and Lexi and Cade were on her left. She focused on Rosie and went into her spiel.

Rosie listened politely as she sipped her coffee. At the end of the speech she put down her mug. "That's a wonderful offer, but here's the deal. I didn't expect either of you to be here during this time, so we have it covered. Matt needs a break and you probably have calls to make. I doubt your business has come to a screeching halt because you flew to Wyoming."

"No, but I'll check in with my office before we start. If I have issues to handle I might have to retract my offer, but nothing was critical when I talked with my assistant yesterday. And I really do want to help."

"I can see that." Rosie beamed at her. "But you and Matt are both excused from cleaning duty."

Matt looked at Geena, his lifted eyebrows clearly saying *I told you so.*

But she wasn't giving up. "You didn't expect us, but here we are, consuming food and taking up space. I'm sure I speak for Matt when I say that we'd feel a whole lot better about our unplanned visit if you'd let us do something for the cause. It won't be a chore for either of us to scrub down a cabin or two. If we hop right on it, maybe we can finish up all four this morning."

"Whoa, there, Geena, ma'am." Cade took off his hat and settled it more securely on his head. "Back up the bus. You gotta leave something for the rest of us. My lady purely loves watching me operate a vacuum cleaner."

Lexi sighed dramatically. "I'll admit it. Nothing's sexier than a man running a vacuum." She fanned herself. "Oh, baby."

"I'd never want to deprive you of that." Geena focused on Lexi, figuring she'd understand the situation even if Rosie balked. "Can we split the job, two cabins for you guys and two for us?"

"Sure, why not?"

"I like it." Matt lifted his coffee mug in Rosie's direction. "Over to you, Mom, but I hope you'll throw in the towel. And the mop and the broom while you're at it."

"Matthew Edward." Rosie frowned at him. "Young women who come to visit Thunder Mountain are welcome to help out a little bit because that's being mannerly. But they're not supposed to wash windows and mop floors."

"Oooh, she said your whole name, bro." Cade rolled his eyes. "Either she's touched or annoyed. It could go either way."

"I'm both." Rosie pulled a tissue from her pocket. "But mostly I'm touched." She dabbed at her eyes and gave them all a teary smile. "When I listen to the four of you arguing for the *privilege* of cleaning the cabins, it gets to me."

"I'll just bet it does," Cade said. "You're probably remembering all the years we tried to argue our way out of doing it."

Rosie laughed and dabbed her eyes some more. "Yes, you certainly did. Very creatively, too."

Cade looked over at Matt. "We were rotten, you know?"

"I know. We should have been more grateful, more willing to—"

"Now, hang on," Herb said. "We're talking about normal boys, here, right?" He put an arm around Rosie. "We would have worried if you'd all gone about your chores with a smile on your face and a song in your heart."

Cade chuckled. "Yeah, that would have been kind of sickening."

"I loved it all," Rosie said. "The arguing, the pranks, the roughhousing. The handpicked bouquets." She winked at Cade.

"Who knew that was poison ivy?"

Herb shook his head and sighed. "Everybody but you, son."

"So many great memories." Rosie looked at Matt. "I'll never forget when you had the lead in *Oklahoma!*"

"Yeah, that was epic," Cade said. "Lining up outside the auditorium an hour early to make sure we sat in front and threatening the younger guys with death if they goofed off during the performance."

"Instead, they were mesmerized," Rosie said. "So was I." She reached over and squeezed Matt's arm. "I knew then you'd make it. I'm pretty sure I told you so."

"Yes, ma'am, you did." Matt's voice was gruff with emotion as he held Rosie's gaze. "Always remembered it."

"Okay, okay." Cade pushed back his chair. "We need to break this up before I start bawling. You don't want to see that, Geena. It gets ugly. So, Mom, is Geena cleared to be part of the cleaning crew?"

"Oh, all right." Rosie got up from the table. "But not in that outfit. Come with me, Geena. While the rest of this bunch tidies up the kitchen, I'll find you some knockabout clothes."

Geena followed Rosie through the living room and

down the hallway. Rosie made a comment about the unseasonably warm weather expected that day and Geena responded to that, but she was more interested in the family pictures lining the hall. A quick glance revealed that most of them were group photos of teenage boys. An older one of a couple in wedding attire had to be Rosie and Herb, but nearby hung a recent wedding picture featuring the couple Geena had met the night before, the ones with the baby.

Rosie looked over her shoulder and paused. "That's Damon and Philomena. They have a baby girl now."

"I know. I met them last night...sort of."

"What do you mean, sort of?" Rosie walked back to stand with her in front of the photograph.

"I was waiting in the driveway debating whether to go up and knock on the door when they came out. They were friendly until they found out who I was. Then they politely offered to escort me back to town."

"Oh, dear. I suppose he was trying to protect Matt. They do stick up for each other. By the way, I called Damon this morning, told him you were staying here and that you were a very nice woman."

"Thank you, Rosie." Geena impulsively gave her a hug and then wondered if she should have. "You'll have to excuse me if that was overly familiar. I just—"

"I love getting hugs." Rosie smiled at her. "The more the better." She gestured to the wall of pictures. "My boys are all good huggers. Some of them came here with the idea that it was unmanly. They got over it."

"I wish I could have seen this place back then. It must have been something."

"I have videos. Maybe while you're here we could have a movie night."

"I would love that." Geena gazed at the two smiling

people who'd been so suspicious of her last night. "Do you have videos of little Sophie?"

"My first grandchild?" Rosie's blue eyes glowed with pride. "You know I do! I'm supposed to get a studio picture for this wall any day now, too."

"I guess you could end up with a lot of baby pictures, couldn't you?"

"I hope so. I'll start a new wall somewhere else in the house if I need to. Now, let's go find you something cool to wear. It'll be a scorcher today." She led the way into a master bedroom containing furniture that was probably as old as the marriage. It wasn't a fancy room, but the bed was neatly made with a white chenille bedspread and the surfaces looked freshly dusted.

"This is my stash of hand-me-downs." Rosie slid back the doors of a large wall closet tightly packed with jeans and shirts hanging from the rod and boots lined up along the floor. "Some kids leave stuff and friends donate things. Sometimes I shop at the thrift store. It's all washed and mended."

"This is amazing, Rosie."

"Thanks." She gave Geena an assessing glance. "I could let you go through them, but it'll be faster if you let me pull some things out. By now I'm pretty good at knowing what will fit and look good."

"All I care about is the fit. Looking good isn't a priority."

Rosie laughed. "Oh, yes, it is. Everyone functions better when they like the way they look. That was one of the first things I learned when I worked in social services. Get someone a decent outfit or two and their entire attitude changes." She quickly chose three shirts and three pairs of jeans. "Not that I think you need an attitude change. Yours is excellent."

"Why, thank you." Geena flushed with pleasure. "What a nice thing to say."

"I know quality when I see it." Rosie handed over the clothes. "Go into the bathroom and try those on while I sort through the boots. That's trickier. Are you about an eight?"

"Nine. I really appreciate this, Rosie."

"I appreciate you going the extra mile." She hesitated. "Nobody likes to be falsely accused, but Matt's more touchy than most. His birth mother used to blame him for all kinds of things he didn't do."

"I'm not surprised. Any mother who can walk away and leave her kid…"

"Did he tell you about that?"

"This morning."

"Good. Then he must trust you, because he doesn't share that with many people."

"I completely understand that he's a very private person. But I'm desperate to find a way to improve his image. I was hoping to use his background, but he doesn't want that for many reasons. Reporters aren't the only ones who could show up here asking questions."

Rosie nodded. "Right. There's Mindy. I've been worried about her ever since he landed that role. She could already be trying to find a way to contact him, but no point in making it easy for her." Rosie patted Geena's arm. "I know this is a knotty problem, but give it a little time. You've only been here since last night."

Geena laughed. "Funny, but it seems much longer. I feel as if I've known you for years."

"That's a lovely compliment." Rosie held her gaze. "I'm going to help you figure this out. Like I said, give it time."

Geena drew a deep breath. "Okay." She chose not to

mention that time wasn't their friend. Even as they stood there discussing the problem, Briana's PR machine was spewing out garbage about Matt. The longer he stayed in hiding, the more likely people would believe all those hateful lies.

After Geena changed into her borrowed clothes, she checked in with Larissa and took notes for the calls she'd make after she finished cleaning. The hour's time difference would be a bonus. Matt, Cade and Lexi had gathered the supplies and were heading to the porch by the time she left her bedroom.

She'd taken everything Rosie had chosen and put on the outfit she liked best. Rosie had also come up with a straw Western hat to keep the sun out of her eyes during the walk to the meadow. Geena had twisted her hair on top of her head and shoved the hat over it.

The boot-cut jeans were a little snug on her, but they were soft and amazingly comfortable. So were the boots Rosie had found. The button-front green plaid shirt was designed to tie at the waist, which gave it a sassy feel. A quick glance in the mirror confirmed that she was finally wearing something that fit the occasion.

Matt's wide smile told her she passed muster. "You look great."

"Thanks." She noticed he'd taken time to shave, which could mean there were kisses in her future. The thought warmed her all over and she worried that her cheeks were pink. Couldn't be helped. "What should I carry?"

"How about a bucket and a mop?" Cade handed them to her and then divided up the rest of the supplies. He was clearly the person in charge.

While Geena had been trying on clothes she'd asked Rosie to fill her in on Cade, whose function wasn't clear to her. It turned out that besides being the ranch fore-man and primary student chaperone, he also taught an academy class in horse psychology. He and Lexi lived in a new log home near the meadow and the pasture, and Rosie had said they couldn't manage without him.

As they all started down toward the meadow, Cade put a hand on Matt's shoulder. "Have you provided Geena with any background on these historic log cabins, bro?"

"He has not," she said. "For one thing, I didn't know they were made of logs. And there are four?"

"Now there are," Cade said. "But originally there were only three. Damon and Phil built the fourth one last sum-mer, so technically only the first three are historic. Es-pecially the first one." He glanced at Matt. "Is it okay if I tell her about the brotherhood?"

"Go for it."

"I should hope you can tell her," Lexi said. "She vol-unteered to clean cabins, for pity's sake. She's working hard to save Matt's reputation. Geena's aces in my book."

Geena flashed Lexi a smile. "Thanks."

"So, the story of the brotherhood." Cade adjusted his grip on a second mop he carried on his shoulder like a rifle. "The first three guys Rosie brought home were Damon Harrison, Finn O'Roarke and me. Damon's—"

"I know who Damon is," she said. "And Finn's the guy who brews the beer we drank last night."

"Exactly. So we created the Thunder Mountain Brother-hood. We had a blood-brother ceremony in the woods where we swore to be straight with everyone, protect the weak and be loyal to one another for life." He stated the pledge without a trace of mockery. He'd obviously believed in the concept then and he believed in it now.

Geena's throat tightened as she imagined three homeless boys pledging to stick together through thick and thin. "That's very cool."

"We thought so, too, but unfortunately we were kind of exclusive. We claimed the first cabin and although it sleeps four, we wouldn't let anybody else in."

Matt shook his head. "Tell me about it. You acted like you were royalty."

"I know. We were obnoxious. But we finally grew up and realized that every guy who shared the experience of living here with Rosie and Herb should be a part of the brotherhood, so now it's official. Everybody's in." He reached over and punched Matt lightly on the arm. "I hope you weren't too traumatized by being excluded for a while, big guy."

"Nah. There's always the cool crowd and then the rest of us."

"Yeah, but today I'm just a lowly cowhand and you're a famous movie star."

Matt grinned at him. "Bite me."

"And get sued by your studio for damaging the goods? No, thanks." He turned back to Geena. "Anyway, that was life in the cabins. Never a dull moment."

"Yeah, and I loved it," Matt said, "despite being lorded over by three megalomaniacs. I used to pretend we were all living on the frontier."

"Which wasn't so far from the truth, considering we had to hike down to the bathhouse in the middle of the night to take care of business. Speaking for myself, I felt like Davy Crockett every time I made that journey."

Geena blinked. "You're kidding, right?"

"No, he's not." Matt looked over at her and grinned. "There's no running water in the cabins."

"Really? How could you manage without indoor bathrooms?"

"Oh, we had indoor bathrooms," Cade said. "We just had to go outdoors to get to 'em. Rain or shine, sleet or snow, down the path we would go."

"Sometimes we had to shovel first, like if we had six feet of snow," Matt said.

"And that was if you could get out your door to shovel." Cade shifted his mop to the other shoulder. "Once the snow was so deep we couldn't pry the doors open. I don't think you'd arrived yet, Matt. Dad dug us out or we would've had to climb out a window. I'll bet we had a good ten feet that year."

She couldn't imagine, but then she was a California girl. "I suppose there are bathrooms in the cabins now, though, for the academy students."

"Nope." Matt shook his head.

"No?"

"They have to do the same thing we did. It's tradition. Toughens them up."

She held out the bucket she was carrying. "So, you're saying in order to mop the floors we have to haul water from the bathhouse?"

"Yes, ma'am."

"Wow, this will be more of an adventure than I thought!"

"You really don't have to do this." Lexi came over to put an arm around her. "Offering to help was a nice gesture, but I'm starting to feel bad about having you do manual labor on your business trip. The three of us can handle it."

"Nice try, but there's no way you're getting rid of me now. I was the kid who never went to camp. I would have loved to—" She stopped in her tracks as the semicircle of four cabins came into view. Nestled in a grassy meadow, they did look as if a family of settlers might have constructed them. Tall pines ringed the meadow and wind sighed through the top branches, making a sound that was hauntingly familiar.

Benches surrounded a fire pit in the middle of the cabin area and the lingering scent of charred logs blended with the aroma of pine. She longed to sit on one of those benches, roast marshmallows and tell ghost stories. Then she'd pile into a cabin with her friends and zip herself into her very own sleeping bag.

"Like it?" Matt's question brought her out of her daydream.

"I don't just *like* it. I *love* it." She realized everyone was watching her with a bemused smile. "This may sound ridiculous, but seeing this meadow is like finding something I didn't know I missed. I can't hear traffic noises or sirens or jackhammers. Maybe I've always needed a place like this in my life. I just didn't know it."

Chapter Nine

Matt had been bowled over by Geena's transformation from city girl to country girl thanks to Rosie's magic closet. Then she'd made those heartfelt comments as she'd stood gazing at the log cabins where he'd spent the happiest years of his life. She'd reacted to the meadow exactly as he had the first time he'd laid eyes on it. She was rapidly turning into the girl of his dreams.

Now he really wanted to take her over to his ranch so she could picture herself going there with him next time he came home. He wouldn't let himself plan too far into the future because that would be foolish. But if he'd found a woman who loved both the film industry and the rural beauty of Wyoming, they could have some fun together.

Once she'd finished exclaiming over the rustic beauty of the cabins and their setting, Cade handed out directions. "We only have one vacuum so we'll have to trade that back and forth. You two can take it first and we'll wash windows until you're done. Then you can wash windows and mop floors while we vacuum. We'll reverse the process for the next two."

"Got it." Matt said.

Cade settled his hat more firmly on his head. "You need to flip the mattresses and look for any items they left behind. After the fall semester we found somebody's credit card."

"Aye, aye, sir." Geena gave him a snappy salute.

Cade's eyes sparkled with laughter. "You'll do, recruit. See you in a few." He and Lexi headed off.

"Nice salute." Matt carried the vacuum cleaner, and Geena took the bucket and mop.

"Learned it in an acting class in case we ever had an audition for a military role. Did you take any classes or are you just a natural born talent?"

"I took community college courses while I was here and enrolled in a couple of acting studios once I hit LA. That was expensive, though, so mostly I watched Westerns because I knew that's where I could shine."

"Lots of John Wayne."

"Yes, ma'am. Plus Steve McQueen, Lee Marvin and every Western Cliff Wallace made. The man can act with his back to the camera. Brando could do that, too. Impressive." He hustled up the steps ahead of her so he could open the door.

"Thank you." She took off her hat and hung it on a hook by the door. "Nice setup."

"It is." Adrenaline pumping, he followed her in and closed the door because he knew from experience it was easier to vacuum that way. Yeah, right. That's why he'd closed the door, so they could clean more efficiently.

Now they were alone, more alone than they'd ever been. The intimacy teased him with possibilities as he stood behind her, trying to breathe normally. Wisps of hair that weren't long enough to fit into her updo curled against the tender skin of her nape. God, how he wanted to kiss her there. Other places, too. Lots of other places. But they had a job to do and there was no telling how fast Cade and Lexi would finish up and come over here.

So he did what most guys did when they couldn't decide whether a move would be appropriate. He babbled about nothing. "Last year I managed a quick visit home after Damon and Phil added the built-in loft beds and desks. We just had regular bunk beds when I was here. This is better. Everybody gets a top bunk and their own private area."

"It's a great idea." She pulled her phone out of her pocket and laid it on the nearest desk. "So we're supposed to vacuum, flip mattresses and look for stray items. Does that cover it until we move into the next phase?"

"Yes, ma'am." She still had her back to him. He thought he'd detected a faint shiver and her shoulders seemed tense, but he could be imagining things. If she was determined to go straight into work mode, so would he.

She swallowed. "Do you want to kiss me first or—"

He put down the vacuum and spun her around so fast she squeaked. "I want to kiss you more than I want to breathe."

"I see." Her green eyes simmered with heat. "Then I won't be needing these." Slowing removing her glasses, she perched them on top of her head where they nestled against her glossy hair.

His heartbeat picked up speed. Shoving back his hat, he pulled her close. Her full lips parted on a sigh. He could almost taste their velvet softness "This is risky."

She wound her arms around his neck. "Is it?"

"Yes, ma'am." He slid his hands over the warm denim covering her backside. For someone so slender, she perfectly filled his cupped hands. His breathing hitched. "Once I start kissing you, I'm liable to forget about cleaning."

She pressed her sweet body against his. "I'll remind you."

"You do that." He took her mouth with the desperation of a starving man. He'd only had a few chances to kiss her, but it seemed that was enough to make him addicted to the supple movement of her lips and the erotic dance of her tongue.

She caught fire immediately and he dove into the richness that was Geena's mouth. His hat fell to the floor. He left it there. He might yearn for a peaceful meadow, but he craved this, to be engulfed in a passion that made him forget his problems, forget everything but the heat of her body and the sound of her moans.

He'd told himself to go slow, but they were alone in this cabin and he wanted...more. Heart pounding, he untied her shirttails and worked his way up the row of buttons. He gave her time to object, but instead she deepened the kiss.

When he'd breached the barrier of her shirt, he discovered the front catch of her bra. What a terrific invention. Anticipation made him clumsy but eventually he flipped open the clasp.

She gasped as his hand closed over her breast.

Breathing hard, he lifted his mouth a fraction from hers. "Do you want me to stop?"

"No."

That one word traveled like a flame along a fuse. Cupping her warm breast, he supported her with his arm and leaned down. His tongue grazed her nipple and she whimpered. Now he knew what that meant.

Slowly he drew her in and listened to the wild sound of her breathing as he hollowed his cheeks and created a rhythm with his mouth and tongue. Her soft whimpers turned into nearly incoherent words.

He lifted his head again. "What?" he murmured. "Tell me."

"I want you so much," she wailed. "But we have to clean!"

Clean. His passion-soaked brain struggled with the concept and finally delivered the bad news. He might have a bed available, although they'd have to climb a ladder to get there, which lacked class. He might have an erection as rigid as the logs used to build this cabin. He might even have a condom in his jeans pocket.

Didn't matter. Instead of making sweet love to Geena, he had to vacuum floors and flip mattresses. Life wasn't even remotely fair.

With a resigned sigh, he released her soft, inviting breast. He didn't dare let go of her completely, though. If she was anywhere near as jacked up as he was, she might lose her balance. He wasn't entirely confident that he wouldn't lose his.

She gulped in air. "I shouldn't have started this. I should have known we couldn't just kiss each other without…"

"Right." He swallowed. "But don't take all the blame. I had a hunch things could get out of control in no time."

"You did?"

"Yes, ma'am. But I was willing to take the risk because kissing you is my new favorite thing."

"Kissing you is mine, too." She took a shaky breath.

"Okay, you can let me go. I'm reasonably steady and I should put myself back together so we can get to work."

He did as she asked and edged away. But he couldn't stop looking at her, although he definitely should because his package strained against his fly. Her creamy breasts trembled with each breath and her nipples, the rich color of burgundy wine, remained taut and eager for his mouth.

Then she gathered all that bounty into the white lace cups of her bra and fastened the catch, depriving him of that particular view. But he still had the tantalizing sight of her unbuttoned blouse and the inviting shadow of her cleavage. He willingly suffered continued pain in his crotch.

Her fingers trembled slightly as she buttoned her shirt and tied the tails in a loose knot. Last of all, she retrieved her glasses from the top of her head and put them on. "All done." She took another deep breath. "Do you want to vacuum or flip mattresses?"

"Neither. I want to strip off all your clothes. Then I want to kiss you until we're both crazy with anticipation. Then I want to make love to you for as long as it takes for both of us to be so satisfied that we can't imagine wanting even one more orgasm."

A fire burned in her green eyes. "That sounds amazing. And we'll do that eventually, I'm sure. But right now, we have to—"

"Clean cabins. I know." He sighed. "I'll flip the mattresses. I'll be done first so I'll haul water and put it on the front stoop for later."

"But I want to haul water."

That made him smile. Apparently she really did look upon this as an adventure. He clenched his hands into fists so he wouldn't reach for her again, because she was just that appealing. "Okay. Want to split some kindling while you're at it?"

"Could I? That would be awesome!"

"Don't see why not." He picked up his hat from the floor and dusted it off. "In fact, there's a dead tree about fifty yards into the forest that Dad wants to cut down."

"There is?" Her eyes widened.

"Yes, ma'am." He stroked a hand over his face so she wouldn't notice his grin. "He mentioned it yesterday. When I fetch the ax from the barn, I could also gas up the chain saw. That way you could—"

"Now you're making fun of me."

"Just a little." He settled his hat on his head. "The thing is, if I don't tease you I'll just have to kiss you again. A woman who's excited about hauling water and chopping wood is tough to resist."

"So is a certain cowboy who took the time to shave before coming out here to clean cabins. I expected you'd still have the scruff."

"And I expected to steal kisses, so the scruff had to go. I don't like giving ladies whisker burn." He backed away. "But I'm staying out of the temptation zone until we get something accomplished. FYI, there's an outlet under each desk."

"Does this happen to be your cabin?"

"It was, in fact, although the built-ins change the look so it feels a lot different. But the outlets stayed the same. Oh, and the vacuum's old and cranky, but everybody's used to it so Mom keeps getting it repaired instead of buying a new one. It's sort of an heirloom."

"I like that." She leaned down and gave the canister vac a pat. "Don't worry, sweetie. I'll treat you with the respect you deserve."

He figured she was kidding, but as he turned over the

mattresses and checked for anything tucked in corners and crevices, he noticed that she used the vacuum efficiently but gently. She didn't bang it against the furniture or drag it by the cord. Every minute he was finding more reasons to like her, more reasons to make her a part of his personal life as well as his professional one.

The mattresses didn't take long and he only found some gum wrappers, a couple of small purple hair clips and a crumpled picture of a popular boy band. Obviously girls had been living in this cabin. Although he'd known all along that the academy was coed, he hadn't grasped the concept that girls might occupy the same cabin where he'd spent his pivotal teenage years. That was more of a shock than the loft beds.

Geena shut off the vacuum. "I found a gold anklet. At least I think it's an anklet." She dangled it from one finger. "Could be a bracelet. I'm glad I didn't suck it up. Her name's engraved on the little gold heart, which means Rosie can mail it back to her." She tucked the delicate gold chain in her jeans pocket.

"I don't think these are worth mailing, though, even if Mom found out who lost them." He showed her the hair clips.

"Nope. Those are easily replaced, but I'll take them. Rosie might want to add them to her stash. I don't know if she has hair doodads, but she might keep some on hand in case the girls lose theirs."

Matt handed them over. "I'll bet she gets a kick out of having girls around for a change."

"She and Herb never considered taking in foster girls, too?"

"Not that I know of. I think when they started with boys, it might have been simpler to stick with that."

"Probably." She shoved the clips in her other pocket

and gazed at him. "You know…" Then she blew out a breath. "Never mind. I should go get the water." She gestured to the vacuum. "Your heirloom awaits. I finished the left side of the room so the right side is all yours. Be right back."

"Wait. You obviously had something to say."

"There's no point. You won't like it."

"I might. You never know."

"Yeah, I do, but I might as well finish my thought. Finding that engraved gold chain brought it home to me that there were teenage girls living here last semester, girls who would go wild if they knew Matt Forrest had been on cleanup duty in the very cabin where they stayed."

A yellow caution light went on in his brain. "Maybe."

"No *maybe* about it. I realize you hate the negative publicity being generated, but—"

"Don't you hate it, too?"

"Yes, absolutely. I'd much rather see positive promo out there for all my clients. But the negative stuff's accomplished one thing. I guarantee most everyone knows who you are, including the teenage girls who lived in this cabin. They'd be super excited to discover you were here in the same space they so recently vacated."

"Even if they think I'm the kind of guy who would seduce a married woman?"

"Like I said before, bad boys are popular, too."

His gut tightened. "I don't want that kind of reputation."

"I know you don't. But I doubt you'd agree to a cute little story about the hot movie star who volunteered his time to clean cabins used by the students of Thunder Mountain Academy."

"You're right. I wouldn't agree to that."

"I can promise you the girls would be over the moon and even the guys might relish the idea that they had a connection to a celebrity, especially one who can ride and rope."

"They might, but I don't want reporters on this ranch invading Mom and Dad's privacy. Or Cade and Lexi's, for that matter."

"I understand." Her gaze was filled with compassion. "But you might end up having to make a choice. If you're determined to protect everyone's privacy, you may be stuck with the bad boy reputation."

The tightness in his gut turned into a slow burn. "I thought you said this was winnable."

"It is, but you may not be willing to do what's necessary to turn this thing around."

Bile rose in his throat. "I won't sacrifice my family for personal gain and that's final."

"I know. I'll be back soon with the water." She put on her straw hat, picked up the bucket sitting beside the door and left.

He turned on the vacuum because then he could swear as loud as he wanted. He'd arrived at the ranch at the age of twelve with a fair number of colorful words in his vocabulary. After hanging out with his foster brothers, he'd added quite a few more. None of the guys used that kind of language around Rosie and Herb, but down in the meadow late at night they used to turn the air blue and laugh like fiends.

This problem was no laughing matter, but swearing still felt like a cleansing activity. He worked his way through his entire repertoire before he started vacuuming. He didn't want to lose his temper with the machine after Geena had treated it with such loving care.

Maybe her assessment of his situation was wrong. But

she was smart and she was capable. Except for her initial reaction to the crisis, he'd been impressed with her grasp of the situation. Unfortunately that might mean she was right about his two choices. Too bad they were sucky and suckier.

Chapter Ten

Cade was on his way over to pick up the vacuum as Geena trudged back carrying the five-gallon bucket that she'd filled about two-thirds full. He didn't notice her and she was happy about that. The bucket was heavier than she'd expected, but she didn't want Cade to figure out that she was struggling and take it off her hands. Matt had given her credit for being strong enough, and she didn't want to admit she wasn't.

Now that she thought about it, chopping wood might not be as easy as she imagined, either. Much as she longed to be a country girl, she was still a city girl playing at country living. That didn't mean she'd have to stay that way, though.

Lugging the water had demonstrated that she was soft. She'd slacked off on her workouts at the gym, but that would change now that she had motivation to develop more upper body strength. She loved this place and wanted to spend more time on this ranch or one like it.

On the way down to the bathhouse, when she hadn't been burdened with a bucket of water, she'd had time to wonder about her visceral reaction to the meadow and the cabins. She couldn't be positive, but she had a vague memory of being in such a place with her father. She would have been less than three, because by that age her mother had taken over her schedule and packed it with activities to mold her into a superstar.

Sometime around then her dad had died while piloting his small plane. Prior to that he might have flown them to some remote spot for a vacation that she barely remembered. Apparently it had made a soul-deep impression on her, though, because she'd felt a connection to these log cabins from her first glimpse of them.

She was grateful for that epiphany and the trip to Wyoming that had made it possible. But her awakening to the beauties of ranching country didn't do anything for Matt's dilemma and she'd come here to help him. She'd had more thoughts about that but wasn't sure how to approach him with her ideas—or whether to approach him at all.

At breakfast, Rosie had talked about all the support she and Herb had received for the academy project. Matt's star power could contribute to the success of the school, perhaps really put it on the map, but reporters would have to be involved. He'd said he didn't want them invading his foster parents' privacy.

But she had no idea how Rosie and Herb felt about it. What if they'd gladly trade a little privacy for the publicity they'd get by aligning themselves with Matt's celebrity status? And what if they were reluctant to ask that of him because they didn't want to risk jeopardizing the privacy he found by coming here?

If it turned out that Matt was protecting Rosie and

Herb while they were protecting him, it was enough to give her a migraine. Or it should have been. But in this setting she couldn't imagine ever having a headache again. The air was blissfully smog-free and she didn't have to endure the cacophony of honking horns and the rhythmic thump of audio systems set to stun.

Los Angeles seemed a million miles away. She'd make those phone calls after this cleaning gig but she wasn't looking forward to talking with the client who'd thrown a tantrum because he hadn't been mentioned in *People* this week. Dealing with Matt wasn't easy, but she'd rather coax someone into the limelight than have to drag a client offstage with a shepherd's crook before they made a complete ass of themselves.

Cade was leaving the cabin with the canister vac in hand as she approached. He put it down and walked to meet her. "Here, I'll take that back for you."

"Thanks, I've got it." She pulled the bucket out of reach so fast she sloshed water on her jeans. Felt kind of good, actually.

His brows lifted. "A little possessive of that bucket, aren't we?"

"Yes. Yes, I am." Sweat trickled down her back. "I carried it all the way here and I intend to finish the job by myself."

"You have grit, Geena Lysander. I like that."

"Thank you." She lowered her voice. "Let me ask you something." She put the bucket down and swallowed a groan of relief.

"Sure."

"Has it occurred to you that linking Matt's name to the academy could be a good thing for business?"

His expression grew wary. "It might have." He moved

a step closer and spoke quietly. "But he needs this place as an escape and that could ruin it for him."

She decided not to address that particular assumption. It could be true, but maybe not if she planned her strategy in advance. "So the thought that Matt could be a draw has crossed your mind."

"Yes, ma'am, but we dismissed it immediately. I hope that's not the road you're heading down."

She noticed his use of *we*. "I'm not heading down any road. I'm still trying to read the map. Matt says he doesn't want your privacy invaded, meaning all four of you—Rosie, Herb, Lexi and you. According to what I'm hearing from him, it's not about his need for privacy. It's about yours."

"See, that's the way he is, always looking out for the people he cares about. Which means we need to look out for him. This situation has made him think that he'd be more of a hindrance than a help."

"But that's not necessarily true."

Cade tugged on the brim of his hat. "No, ma'am, but as long as he thinks it is, then Thunder Mountain can continue to be his sanctuary. Which is fine with us."

"When you say *us*, do you mean the four of you?"

"Uh, there's a few more than that involved."

"Who?"

He hesitated.

"If you don't mind my asking."

"Guess not. You've been trustworthy so far."

"Cade, I care about Matt. I'd never do anything to hurt him."

He met her gaze and seemed to be evaluating what to say. Finally he nodded. "Okay. Ever since Matt got this part, we've recognized his potential to help the academy. The primary group on site includes Mom, Dad, Lexi and me, plus Damon and Phil. Then there's Ben Radcliffe, who teaches saddle making for us, and his wife, Molly, who set up the curriculum. Finn's wife, Chelsea, is in marketing, so she immediately saw the possibilities, but she also knows that Matt's a private guy who cherishes this ranch. The upshot is that no one's said a word to him about helping to publicize the academy."

"So you guys are miles ahead of me. I had no idea."

"And now you know."

"I do. Thanks for trusting me with this."

"You can't tell him."

"I won't."

He smiled. "And now you'd better take that water where it belongs before he sends out a search party."

"Aye, aye, sir!" She snapped him another salute and picked up her bucket. She was pleased that he chuckled as she walked away. Cade was one of the good guys. In fact, they all sounded terrific and she wished she could meet the rest of the brotherhood.

When she reached the cabin, she left the bucket on the cement stoop and opened the door.

Matt had taken off his hat and had his back to her as he vigorously cleaned the inside of a window. He didn't turn around. "I was about to go looking for you."

"It was more of a challenge than I thought." But watching his tight buns flex inside well-washed denim and his back muscles shift beneath his white T-shirt was reward enough.

"Did you find the outside faucet?" He leaned over to rub a spot near the bottom of the window.

Lordy. "I did." She paused to clear the lust from her throat. "After I figured out that getting water from one of the sinks or from the shower wasn't practical, I went looking for a better alternative."

"Should've known you would." He gave the window one last swipe and turned around. "Did you run into Cade? He just left a bit ago with the vacuum."

"Yep, I saw him." She hoped her expression didn't give anything away.

"The windows over there were a lot dirtier than these, apparently." He gazed at her. "Which is lucky for us or Cade would have shown up a *lot* earlier to fetch the vacuum."

"You mean early enough to catch us…kissing?" Matt had done a lot more than kiss her, and she wouldn't mind having him repeat the process now that they were alone again.

"Yes, ma'am. Sorry about that. I forgot he's amazingly fast at windows."

"You also were looking proficient at the window-cleaning gig when I walked in here." She still had a buzz going. "How fast is Cade at vacuuming?"

His eyes darkened. "Too damned fast, I'm afraid." He tossed down the towel he'd been using on the window and came toward her. "Especially when you look at me like that. But I don't dare grab hold of you. I know what will happen." He reached out and brushed a damp strand of hair from her cheek and sucked in a breath. "There's something so sexy about a woman who's been outside getting sweaty."

She laughed, although her heart was pounding. "I can't imagine what."

"Can't you?" He brushed his knuckles lightly over her throat. "Your skin's already nice and warm, plus it's damp, which makes it so easy to slide my hand—"

"All right, I get it." She gulped and stepped back.

"Your glasses are fogged up again."

"I know." She quickly cleaned them on the tail of her

shirt. "You're right, we can't do this. Cade and Lexi will show up and find us rolling around on the floor."

"Rolling? Really?" His smile had a definite touch of wickedness. "I don't know about you, but I find it's a lot nicer if you stay put."

She groaned. "We need to start mopping this floor before I say to heck with what Cade and Lexi find us doing. Are you finished with the windows?"

"I'm finished with the inside. If you're willing to mop, I'll go take off the screens and do the outside."

"I'd rather have you do *me*."

"Yes, ma'am." He winked at her before scooping up the towel he'd dropped and snagging the spray bottle of window cleaner. "So would I." He went out the door, transferred the bucket from the stoop to the inside, and left her to work out her frustrations with some vigorous mopping.

Matt vowed that he'd concentrate on the windows. He'd taken off the screens without once looking inside the cabin. Then he'd washed an entire window while managing to ignore whatever was happening on the opposite side of the glass. Feeling noble and in control, he'd decided it wouldn't hurt to take a quick peek inside to see how Geena was coming along with her mopping.

He was still watching her when Cade clapped him on the shoulder, causing him to jump and drop the spray bottle. Luckily it was plastic. When he turned to confront a grinning Cade, he discovered Lexi was there, too, looking highly amused.

Matt glared at both of them, but mostly at Cade for startling him. "You shouldn't sneak up on a guy with a loaded spray bottle in his hand. I could've hit you in the face with a blast of window cleaner. That stuff has to be bad for your eyes."

"Couldn't resist, bro. But I regret to inform you that most women don't go for the Peeping Tom routine. If she catches you doing it, I guarantee she'll think it's creepy that you're staring in the window while she's mopping the floor. You'll lose points, bro, major points."

"But she's not just mopping. She's tap dancing while she does it."

"Are you kidding me?"

"Nope. Take a look."

Cade moved to the window. "I'll be damned. C'mere, Lex. This reminds me of those old black-and-white movies Mom likes."

Lexi walked over and stood on tiptoe. "I can't really see."

"Okay, here you go." Cade crouched down. "Get on my shoulders."

"You know, I don't think—"

"Do it. This is worth the price of admission."

"I hope she doesn't glance our way and see this." Lexi climbed on Cade's shoulders and he slowly got to his feet. "Oh, wow. She really is tap dancing. In cowboy boots, no less, and wearing her hat! I wonder if she has music. I can't hear anything. Maybe she has music on her phone."

"Maybe."

"Well, that's just cool. Look at her go! She's—uh-oh. She saw us. Now she'll probably quit."

Matt expected that, too. But after giving them a smile and a wave, she continued with her routine as she worked her way toward the cabin door. When she finished, she spun back toward them and bowed. They all applauded and Matt whistled through his teeth.

"Let's meet her at the door." Lexi hopped down and they walked around to the front of the cabin.

Geena came out holding the bucket with the mop handle sticking out of it. She was breathing hard and her cheeks were bright pink. Matt couldn't remember ever seeing a prettier sight, and he'd spent three years in the land of gorgeous women.

They all clapped and cheered, which made her roll her eyes and laugh. Setting down the bucket, she executed another little dance step on the concrete stoop and swept off her hat in a dramatic gesture, dislodging the pins in her hair. It tumbled out of its arrangement.

"That was *awesome*," Lexi said. "No wonder you caught on to the dance moves so quickly last night. You're a pro!"

"Sadly, I'm not. I haven't tapped in a while, so I'm pretty rusty and so out of shape."

Matt picked up the bucket and mop. He was willing to argue that point. He loved her shape. And her hair, which hung in glorious waves to her shoulders. He longed to comb it back with his fingers, cup her head in both hands and tilt it so he could kiss that smiling mouth.

"Would you please hold this for a sec while I fix my hair?" She handed him her hat.

"Sure." He felt like telling her to leave it down because it looked sexy that way. He thought better of saying that out loud.

Drawing a deep breath, she retrieved the scattered pins and used them to anchor her hair on top of her head again. "The mop reminded me of a number we put together when I was taking dance. We combined moves from the Gene Kelly mop dance and Fred Astaire's routine with a broom. You may not have seen either of those since they're from really old movies."

"I have," Cade said. "So have Damon and Finn. When we first came to the ranch, before the cabins were built, we used to sit in the living room and watch those musicals with Mom. She's crazy about them. She'd go nuts if you did a tap number for her."

"I'd probably be too self-conscious to give a planned performance. I don't even have the right shoes." She took back her hat and put it on.

"That's what made it so impressive," Lexi said. "You weren't wearing tap shoes. Did you have music playing?"

"Just in my head. I thought nobody was watching. Then I saw you guys at the window and my training kicked in. My dance teacher drummed into us that you never stop in the middle of a number when you have an audience. No matter what, the show must go on."

"I'm glad you didn't stop." Matt had been smitten before, but after that dance routine he was completely dazzled. He could manage a two-step and a waltz without a problem, but he didn't have the dedication to learn something as complicated as tap. Consequently, he admired the hell out of someone who'd had the determination to get good at it.

He had to laugh when he thought about the earnest conversation he'd had with Geena on the porch last night. They'd both announced that now was not the time to have a serious relationship. He'd been of a similar mindset when he told Cade and Lexi he didn't want Rosie launching into matchmaking mode.

On paper, the timing of his sudden interest in Geena couldn't be worse. His career was finally off to a promising start, but the film business was notoriously unstable. An actor could go from fame to obscurity in the blink of an eye.

Asking someone to share the ride when the journey

was wildly uncertain wasn't fair. His head knew that, but his heart wasn't listening. He was falling for this amazing woman at an alarming rate and getting serious sounded like a terrific idea. If Rosie had any advice on how to turn a temporary fling into something more permanent, he was ready to hear it.

Chapter Eleven

The four of them ended up working together on the last two cabins, which was fine with Matt. He got a kick out of the way Geena interacted with Cade and Lexi, as if she'd known them forever. They treated her the same way. Apparently they recognized qualities in each other that made friendship easy.

Besides, he'd given up the idea of more sexy interludes with her during this cleaning gig. Too much risk of being interrupted and he was feeling increasingly grubby. Before he held her again he needed a shower and a closer shave than he'd managed early this morning.

On the way back to the house Cade got into a conversation with Geena about old movies, and that gave Matt a chance to mention the upcoming trail ride to Lexi.

"Should be fun."

"I've never taken someone out who hasn't been on a horse. Is that a stupid idea? You were planning to give her a lesson and I don't want to jump the gun if you think she needs a lesson first."

"Cade mentioned that she seemed really comfortable with the horses this morning. I'm not saying a lesson wouldn't be helpful at some point, but greenhorns take trail rides all the time without any prior experience." Lexi smiled. "She has to be coordinated or she wouldn't be able to tap dance."

"What's that?" Geena called over to them. "Are you two talking about me?"

"Yes, ma'am." Matt glanced at her. "I wanted to get Lexi's opinion on our trail ride plan. She thinks it'll be fine."

"Good, because I think so, too, especially if we meander over to Matt's ranch and meander back."

Cade laughed. "Considering you're taking Navarre and Isabeau out in the middle of a warm day, you won't get them to do anything *but* meander."

"And that's perfect for a beginner like me. If Lexi and I can find the time for a lesson while I'm here, great. After I know more I'll try going a little faster."

Lexi pulled out her phone and consulted the screen. "How about first thing tomorrow morning? I don't have anything scheduled until ten." She grinned. "And now that you're used to getting up at dawn, we could work in a quick lesson before breakfast."

"That would be great. Thanks."

"Lexi's phone reminded me of something," Cade said. "Geena, you'd better take yours on the ride."

"I would, anyway, in case my assistant needs to get in touch."

"That's good, because last I heard, hotshot here stowed his in the bottom of a dresser drawer."

"No worries, bro." Matt looked over at him. "I'd already planned to unearth it for the ride."

"Well, good. Is the battery charged?"

Matt sighed. "Yes, Cade, the battery's charged."

"I'm delighted to hear it, because a gentleman would never take a lady on a trail ride without bringing his fully charged phone in case of an emergency."

"You won't have an emergency," Lexi added quickly. "But it's always good to be prepared."

"Have either of you seen my new place?" He didn't want to spoil the ambience by taking Geena to see peeling paint and rotting wood.

"Sorry, bro." Cade shook his head. "Haven't had the time. Mom and Dad said it has a lot of promise and that you got a good price on it."

"Is that code for *it's a dump but with a ton of work it'll be reasonably okay*?"

"I don't think it's a dump," Lexi said. "They wouldn't have let you buy it if they thought that. But I wouldn't expect it to look like a page out of a guest-ranch brochure, either."

"No worries," Geena said. "It's exciting that you bought a ranch, regardless of what it looks like."

"Yeah, it is." He hadn't cared what it looked like, either, until he'd invited her over there. But he wouldn't worry about it. How bad could it be?

"I have a question," Cade said. "Assuming you get it fixed up and maybe buy yourself a couple of horses, who's gonna take care of the place while you're in Hollywood being famous?"

"I'll need to hire someone. Got any ideas?"

"I might. Let me give it some thought."

"I wouldn't mind having somebody lined up before I go back."

"And when will that be?"

"Not sure yet."

"Don't forget you have that appearance for *Preston's Revenge* next week," Geena said.

"Right."

"And I booked you into two morning talk shows after that."

He nodded. "They're on my calendar." At one time he'd been excited about those publicity gigs.

"Don't worry." Her voice softened. "We'll schedule some coaching sessions before you do any of it. But I'll need my video equipment to do it right. I'd like you back in LA by Monday, at the latest."

"No worries," Cade said. "We can locate a caretaker for the ranch before then." He turned to Geena. "Can you stay until Monday?"

"I can if I absolutely have to, but I'd hate to think this issue will drag on that long. Surely we'll find a way to put a cork in it soon."

Matt blew out a breath. "Or I could just accept my new image as a bad boy and move on."

"Whoa, what?" Cade stopped walking and stared at him.

"It's an option. I don't have to apologize because that kind of guy wouldn't. If I give up worrying about my white hat image, I also don't have to put my family in front of a camera to testify that I'm some kind of paragon. Like I said, it's an option. I'm thinking about it."

Cade shook his head. "Well, you can stop thinking about it. We're the Thunder Mountain Brotherhood." His eyes took on a steely glint. "When someone attacks, we don't just roll over."

"We also don't put our loved ones in harm's way." Matt held his gaze. "If you think that by staying silent and taking the rap I'll be dishonoring the brotherhood, then I'll resign from—"

"Aw, hell, I didn't mean that! I'm asking you not to give up, okay? I swear we'll find a way out of this that will work for everybody."

"Like what?"

"I don't know yet. But remember that you're not alone and I'm not just talking about the folks, Lexi and me. The brotherhood is with you, all of us, and I'm thinking we may not have tapped into that firepower like we should be doing. Let me make some calls, see if we can set up a Skype thing tonight."

Emotion clogged Matt's throat and he had to clear it before he could speak. "That...that would be..."

"Fun?"

"That, too." He smiled. "Thanks. Even if nothing comes of it, I—"

"Something will come of it." Cade took a deep breath. "But I'd love for you and Geena to take a nice ride over to your new ranch and forget all about it for a few hours. Think you can do that, cowboy?"

Matt looked into his brother's eyes and saw a strength and determination that gave him more hope than he'd had in days. "Yeah, we can do that."

An hour later, Geena had made her phone calls and dealt with the prima donna. Although he was difficult to work with, he was a popular actor and gave her fledgling company a lot of street cred. Matt had the potential to do the same thing, which was why she'd agreed to work with him. And, bonus, he wasn't a prima donna.

She envisioned great things for him in the future, which would be good for both of them. Having a personal relationship added an element of risk, though, and she wasn't blind to the danger. If they developed issues, that would affect their business arrangement. She'd decided to think positively on that score.

For now, their personal relationship was uppermost in her mind because she was on her way to his ranch and riding a horse for the first time in her life. Except something about that felt familiar. Watching Isabeau's ears flick back and forth, and listening to the creak of the saddle triggered a memory.

They'd left the ranch property single file but now rode side by side down a dirt road that Matt had told her belonged to the Forest Service. Tall pines shaded a strip along the edge, but the sun was directly overhead. She felt it on her back and shoulders, but she was a California girl who was used to it.

She'd worn another pair of the jeans Rosie had loaned her, but she'd decided her white stretch tank would work for the ride if she slathered on sunscreen. She was also glad for the straw hat.

Lexi had given her a few pointers when she'd mounted up. She was supposed to keep her heels down and her back straight. Although she held the reins loosely in one hand, she had Lexi's permission to hang on to the saddle horn with the other as much as she wanted if it gave her a sense of security.

It did. At first the sensation of sitting astride a large animal had been unnerving and she'd hung on for dear life. Gradually, though, she'd become used to the rocking motion and she'd relaxed her grip on the horn.

As they rode, Matt described the scene in winter when everything was covered in a blanket of snow. Last semester the academy students had reconditioned an old sleigh under Phil's supervision, and now sleigh rides had been added to the list of activities. A white Christmas wasn't guaranteed in Wyoming, but Matt was hoping for one this year, and time off so he could spend the holiday at Thunder Mountain.

Geena loved hearing details like that and secretly hoped he would invite her along on such a trip. But she suspected he was making small talk because he'd promised to banish negative thoughts for the rest of the afternoon. Cade hadn't made her promise, but she'd do her best, too.

Cade's plan to rally his brothers brought tears to her eyes every time she thought about it. No matter what happened as a result, she'd never forget the love and pride in his voice as he'd reminded Matt that the Thunder Mountain Brotherhood had his back.

"You're looking good over there," Matt said. "How does it feel?"

"Believe it or not, like I've done this before."

"But you said you'd never ridden."

"I haven't, not like this. But Isabeau's head bobbing in front of me is very familiar."

"A pony ride, maybe?"

"No, I wasn't sitting on the horse. I was in somebody's lap." She glanced over at him. "You know what? I'll bet when I was very little, like, maybe two and a half, my dad held me while we went riding. I think the two of us might have taken a vacation together. I'm guessing there were log cabins and horses. That would explain the déjà vu."

"Where is he now?"

"He crashed his private plane when I was about three. No survivors."

"Damn."

"It's sad, and I sure wish it hadn't happened, but the truth is I barely remember him. He and my mom had already divorced by then. I'd love to ask her if he and I went on that kind of vacation, but she gets weepy when his name comes up."

"So, she still misses him."

"Yep. Once I went in her closet to try on her shoes and found an old love note from him tucked in the toe of sparkly red heels I'd never seen her wear. It's cool to know they were once in love, even if they didn't stay together."

"That is cool."

She heard the wistfulness in his voice and regretted having mentioned it. He didn't know who his father was, let alone whether his mom and dad had been in love. Likely not. Time to leave the past and concentrate on the present. "I have to say you're looking quite manly mounted up on your trusty steed."

"Oh?" He seemed to mentally pull himself back from wherever her story had sent him. "Thank you, ma'am." He winked at her and touched the brim of his Stetson. "Mighty kind of you to say so."

Her heart lurched. He was such a great guy. She'd never forgive Briana for making a move on him and creating this horrible scenario.

"Something wrong?" Matt's voice cut through her thoughts.

"No, why?"

"You're scowling."

She slowly breathed out and relaxed her facial muscles. So much for honoring Cade's wish that they could forget the problems and enjoy the afternoon. "Sorry."

"Care to tell me what you were scowling about?"

She turned to him with a sunny smile. "No."

"Okay."

He probably knew what she'd been thinking. What a waste. The day was beautiful and she was riding along-side a gorgeous cowboy who truly deserved to wear a white hat, even though currently his was brown. He'd showered and put on a clean white T-shirt and jeans. She suspected, from the scent of cologne drifting her way and the nick on his square jaw, that he'd shaved again.

"How much longer is the ride?"

He laughed. "Is that a version of *Are we there, yet?*"

"Kind of. I have a strong urge to kiss that little spot where you cut yourself shaving."

"Only that one spot?"

Just like that, he'd managed to jump-start her libido with a single teasing question. "Um, now that you mention it…"

"If you hadn't been so keen on seeing my ranch, we'd be making out on a picnic blanket this very minute."

"Where?" The eagerness in her voice was embarrassing, but she couldn't help it.

"A grassy meadow I know about. We passed it a ways back."

She glanced over her shoulder.

"No, ma'am, you can't see it from here and we're not heading back. We're closer to my ranch than we are to the meadow, and I have some special places I want to kiss once I get the chance. Wanna hear where they are?"

"Better not." Whew. She squirmed in the saddle and Isabeau snorted. "Hey, cowboy, you'd better dial back the sexy before I swoon and fall right off this horse."

Matt's low chuckle sent shivers down her spine. "You started it." He looked over at her and smiled. "It won't be long now. The back entrance is up yonder." He pointed to a weathered gate between two thick posts.

"I see it." *Up yonder.* She didn't remember him using phrases like that in LA. Being here really brought out the country in him and she loved that, too. "So we're going in the back way?"

"That's the best route for horses. If you're driving you take the paved road to the front gate. Either way, it's not too far from Thunder Mountain."

"Who knows you bought this place?"

"My family, you, the bank and the real estate agent. I'm guessing some other people in town know because word gets around when a ranch is bought or sold."

"You didn't tell any of your friends in LA?"

"Nope. They're still struggling financially, like I was six months ago. Mentioning that I'd bought a ranch seemed like bragging. I didn't bring it up."

That was so like him, thinking of someone else's feelings instead of his excitement about a major purchase.

"It'll be a while before I'm ready to invite anybody here, anyway." He halted Navarre in front of the sagging gate and swung down from the saddle. "Let's hope the house looks better than this gate." He took a key from his pocket and opened the padlock on a thick chain wrapped around both the gate and the post.

He gently pushed the gate inward as the hinges squeaked and the wood groaned. Then he stepped back and motioned her forward. "After you."

She nudged Isabeau in the ribs the way Lexi had shown her and the mare slowly trudged through the opening. Then she looked back at Navarre and whinnied. "She's not liking this," Geena said.

"I know she doesn't. Hey, Izzy, it's okay. We won't leave your boyfriend behind." Matt led Navarre through and closed the gate.

"See? You do think of them as a couple." Geena turned in her saddle so she could watch him mount up. So smooth. She'd love a video but her phone was in her saddlebag and he wouldn't want her to take one, anyway.

"Hard not to think of them as a couple with those

names. But as you can probably tell, Izzy's not a very liberated lady. Now that we're headed down a one-lane path, she'll want Navarre to lead."

"Fine with me. You should get the first look at your ranch house, anyway. You must be excited to finally see it."

He pulled alongside her and tipped back his hat. "Not nearly as excited as I am about what's going to happen when we get there."

She gulped. "Careful. I might swoon."

"In a few minutes you can do that all you want. I've been thinking about how this will likely play out."

"I thought…" She drew in a quick breath. "I thought we'd decided to clean off a spot on the floor and put down the blanket." It was tied behind his saddle and she'd been extremely aware of it the entire ride.

His hot glance traveled over her, igniting fires wherever it touched. "Let's be honest. We'll never make it into the house, let alone have the presence of mind to sweep the floor and lay down a blanket."

"Oh." Her brain turned to mush. "So what…what should we do?"

"Tie the horses, take this blanket—" He gave it a quick pat. "And find a nice patch of grass."

"Out…outside?"

"No one will be there but us." His gaze searched hers. "But if you don't want to—"

"Yes." She was very nearly panting and could barely speak. "I want to."

Chapter Twelve

Matt almost pulled her off her horse so they could execute the plan right then and there. But that would lack significance. He wanted her desperately, but this wasn't just about sex.

He gave the brim of his hat a determined downward tug. "Then let's go." He tapped Navarre with his boot heels. Snorting, the horse set out at a brisk walk, and Matt looked over his shoulder to see how Geena was handling the faster pace. "You okay?"

"Never better!" She'd tightened her grip on the saddle horn but she hadn't lost either of her stirrups. Some of her hair had escaped from under her hat and her skin was flushed a becoming shade of pink. She was smiling.

He couldn't stop looking at that smile. Emotions crowded his chest until he wondered if it would break wide open from the pressure. Even when he faced forward again so he could see where the hell he was going, her smile stayed with him. He thought of what was about to happen and his hands began to shake.

It seemed he was nervous. As the leading man in a major motion picture, he'd made pretend love to a big-time movie star in front of a stage crew and several cameras, but he was afraid he'd mess this up. He'd also made love for real with several women since losing his virginity at seventeen, but he'd never felt as if his whole future depended on it. Maybe taking her on a blanket outside wasn't a good idea.

Maybe he should wait for a bed, clean sheets and a cool breeze through curtained windows. Because when it was all over, he needed to see that smile. He wanted that more than anything he'd ever wished for in his entire crazy life.

He was so absorbed in his inner debate that he rode right past the fence enclosing a pasture before he realized what he was looking at. Not much of the fence was still standing, so maybe he could be excused for missing it.

At that point the horse trail ended and he rode into an open space between the barn on his right and the house about thirty yards away on his left. *His house.* He'd never owned anything of value except an old pickup he'd sold before he'd left for LA.

He pulled Navarre to a halt and pivoted the horse in order to watch Geena coming toward him on Isabeau. Damn, that woman was so beautiful it made his throat hurt. And there was that heart-stopping smile again, one that he returned because, just like that, his doubts were gone.

What happened in the future didn't matter anymore. She was here today, and as eager to be his lover as he was to be hers. That was more than some men were given in a lifetime. His heart pounded and heat rushed to his groin. Debate over.

Her green eyes sparkled. "Just think, Matt. This is your land."

"Hard to believe."

"The barn looks sturdy."

He laughed. "Nice way to put it." He angled his head toward the house and turned Navarre back in that direction. "Let's go see if the house looks sturdy, too." Along the way they passed some clumps of weeds but so far not much in the way of grass. He hoped they'd find some in the front yard. Although he'd seen grass growing in the pasture, that wasn't the ambience he was after.

"I'm sure the house is sturdy," she said. "Like Lexi said, your folks wouldn't let you buy a place that had major structural flaws."

"And it wasn't like I could afford a showplace. Not if I wanted acreage to go with the house and barn."

"How many acres do you have?"

"Almost twenty-five."

"That sounds huge!"

"Not by Wyoming standards. But it's fine for me and a couple of horses."

"And whoever you hire to watch the place while you're gone."

"True." If he wanted horses, someone would have to live on the ranch year-round. Funny how he'd imagined bringing her back here in a few months for some private time, but unless he asked his hired hand to take off for a couple of days, he and Geena wouldn't be alone, after all.

They were now, though. Except for the birds chattering and the low sigh of a breeze, the place was quiet. Intimate. He looked over at her and she was looking right back. Her throat moved in a slow swallow.

"Nervous?"

"Some. Mostly excited."

"Me, too." As they approached the house from the side, he could see the large tree in front near the porch. In the picture it had been leafless, but now it was budding out in response to the warm weather. And, hallclujah, under the tree was a nice little patch of spring grass that might not have been there a week or two ago.

He spared a quick glance for the house, which looked fine, as Geena had predicted. It had been painted recently, but mustard yellow wouldn't have been his first choice. Didn't matter. Paint was cheap.

He rode up to the side railing of the porch and dismounted, anticipation making him stumble slightly. Navarre looked back at him. "Yeah, I know. Pathetic."

He turned to Geena, who'd pulled Isabeau to a stop. "You can park her next to Navarre. I'll help you down." He looped Navarre's reins loosely around the railing.

"I can get down by myself."

"Yes, ma'am, I know you can." He walked around to Isabeau's left side, took the mare's reins and wrapped them around the railing. "But you might need me to steady you a little bit, in case you're shaky." What a laugh. If anyone was shaky, he was. He needed to touch her. The sooner he could do that, the sooner his world would start making sense again.

"You could be right about that." She held tight to the saddle horn and swung her leg over Isabeau's rump.

Spanning her waist with his hands, Matt guided her descent until she had both feet on the ground. Then he didn't want to let go.

"Matt, I'm okay. You can—" She gasped as he spun her around.

"To hell with the blanket." He scooped her into his

arms and carried her over to the grass. Her hat fell off somewhere along the way, but she didn't seem to notice.

Instead, she wound her arms around his neck. She was breathing fast, and little puffs of warm air tickled his throat. He couldn't look down to see if she was okay with this because in his current state he might run smack into the tree trunk.

Somehow he managed to lay her on the fragrant grass without injuring either of them. He was coiled tight as a buckboard spring, but as he looked at her lying there, he realized he should find a safe place for her glasses. Leaning over her, he gently removed them, took off his hat and dropped her glasses inside.

"Thanks." Her voice was husky.

"Anytime." Setting his hat aside, he looked into her eyes. "If you—" He paused to suck in some air. "If you want me to get the blanket, or if you want anything to be different, you'd better tell me now."

"I want *you*." She grasped his face in both hands and pulled him down for an open-mouthed kiss that fried what was left of his brain.

Operating solely on instinct, he pushed up the stretchy cotton of her tank and found another front-catch bra under there. Instead of taking anything off, he simply moved the material aside. Then he broke away from her kiss so he could savor her beautiful breasts.

She moaned and arched into his caress, and at last she begged for more. She was very specific about what she wanted and he loved that she was so bold, loved that her hunger matched his. His cock swelled in response.

First her boots had to go. Next he pulled off her jeans and panties in one smooth motion. Earlier, caught in the frenzied dance of anticipation, he'd fumbled the simplest tasks, but now he was extremely focused.

His gaze swept over her as he knelt in the grass. He wanted the bra and tank top out of the way, too. "Lift your arms."

Holding his gaze, she raised them over her head and he removed the last of her clothes. She lay there panting as the scent of crushed grass and arousal flowed around them. Sunlight filtered by the new leaves created a dappled pattern on her smooth skin—pale where the sun's rays had been blocked by her swimsuit and golden where the sun had been allowed to kiss her.

"You look…like a goddess."

"I feel like one." Her green eyes glowed with passion. "And I command you to strip down, cowboy."

Wordlessly he reached back, grabbed his T-shirt with both hands and pulled it over his head. The slight breeze felt good on his bare chest.

She brushed her fingers over his chest hair. "They didn't make you shave."

"No." His heart thudded wildly. How had she guessed he was sensitive there? "They were going for—" He gasped as she gently pinched his nipple. "Historical accuracy."

"I'm glad. I like this look." She ran her fingertips down the strip of dark hair that disappeared under his belt buckle. "But you're still overdressed."

"I can fix that." Soon his boots and socks were history and he shucked his jeans and briefs in record time. But he remembered to take that all-important item from his pocket before he tossed his pants aside. He tore open the packet and rolled on the condom.

At last. Moving over her, he flattened his palms on the cool grass and settled between her thighs. His voice was tight with the strain of keeping himself in check. "You probably think I'm crazy."

"Not crazy. Creative." Her voice trembled, but her hands were steady as she caressed his shoulders and the tense muscles of his back. "You turn me on, Matt."

"Lucky me." He eased forward.

"Lucky us." She welcomed him with liquid heat and delicious friction that made him groan with pleasure.

His first impulse was to hide his reaction to the intense feeling of connection as he slid into her. He was good at hiding his emotions. Usually it was the safest course of action.

But this time, when she so obviously trusted him, it seemed wrong. Looking into her eyes, he masked nothing as he slowly began to stroke.

Neither did she. He drank in the passion, tenderness and joy shining in her gaze. And, ah, she was so eager. Her soft moans of pleasure told him that she wanted this with every fiber of her being. Gradually he picked up the pace.

Her fingertips dug into the muscles of his back as she rose to meet him. "Matt… *Matt.*"

"I'm here." He pushed in tight and paused, his gaze locked with hers. "Right here."

"I know." Her body grew taut. "I *know.*" She began to quiver and her eyes darkened, but she held his gaze as her climax swept through her. Gasping his name, she arched upward as if inviting him to plunge deeper.

His control snapped. With a roar of triumph, he thrust hard into her pulsing channel and welcomed an orgasm that electrified every muscle from his scalp to his toes. He nearly blacked out from the force of it.

Panting, he fought to keep himself braced on his outstretched arms. Gradually his vision cleared enough that he could see her face again. His wish had been granted. She was smiling.

* * *

In Geena's experience, happiness was difficult to pin down. No more. Happiness was looking into Matt's blue eyes and seeing the wonder of their shared climax reflected there. Happiness was feeling soft, damp grass against her bare skin and a gentle breeze brushing her heated cheeks. Happiness was realizing that today, in this place, with this man, she'd discovered a human connection so strong that she'd never again settle for less.

"I love it when you smile like that." He traced her lower lip with the pad of his thumb. "I almost hate to kiss you and give up my view of that smile." He leaned closer. "But I will."

"Please do." Oh, yes, and happiness was kissing someone who put his heart and soul into it. She did the same, which made for a kiss that was long, satisfying and... arousing? Incredibly, she wanted him again. Judging from the evidence, he would be happy to comply.

Lifting his head, he gazed down at her. "You're powerful medicine, lady. I feel like I'm seventeen again."

"Not me. I never had this much fun when I was seventeen."

"Come to think of it, neither did I. I was clueless."

"I'm here to tell you that's no longer the case."

"Thank you, ma'am. Is that a green light?"

"That's a hell yes."

"Hallelujah." He brushed a quick kiss over her mouth. "Don't go away."

"Not a chance." After he left she watched the tender green leaves above her dancing in the sunlight. She hadn't felt like dancing since she'd quit at eighteen. Until today. Until Matt.

Then he was there, moving between her thighs, his gaze warmer than the sun.

Her pulse rate shot up. "That was a fast turnaround, cowboy." Stroking both hands down his back, she cupped his firm buns.

"I was highly motivated." He nibbled on her mouth. "Didn't want you to get bored and leave."

"Like that was going to happen."

"You never know. But it's too late now." He entered her with one swift thrust. "Gotcha." Then he captured her low moan of surrender with an open-mouthed kiss.

The first time had been wonderful. She'd doubted that he could improve on something so perfect, but she hadn't stopped to think that he'd have more staying power the second time around. Lordy, did he know how to use staying power.

He drove her to the brink of insanity and then slowed the pace, teasing her with a leisurely yet erotic motion that kept her at a fever pitch without sending her over the edge. When she began to beg, he finally ramped up the action and she was enveloped in a whirlpool of pleasure. She expected him to follow her there, but instead he kept going.

"Matt?" Gasping, she looked up.

"You're amazing." His breathing was labored but his smile was filled with joy. "I'm having...the time of my life." He gulped for air. "Wrap your legs around me. You're going to come again."

She followed his directions, and sure enough, she swirled into another orgasm. Then he claimed his release, shuddering as a cry rose from deep in his throat. His chest heaved and his biceps trembled, but he remained braced on his outstretched forearms.

Tightening her hold on him, she tugged gently. "Come here."

He shook his head but there was no mistaking the yearning in his eyes. "I don't want to crush you."

"You won't. Lie with me."

A hint of vulnerability flashed in his eyes, but he eased down until he was nestled against her. Sighing, he laid his head on her shoulder. "Tell me if I'm too heavy."

"You're not." She combed her fingers through his damp hair. "You're perfect."

"You are, too."

She listened to his breathing as it slowly evened out. She had no idea what came next in what seemed to be turning into an actual relationship. Sure, making love always changed the dynamic. But she hadn't expected it to change her entire view of the future. Now she couldn't imagine hers without Matt.

Chapter Thirteen

As they lay together, sated and relaxed, Geena's stomach growled.

Matt chuckled. "I heard that. I'll fetch our lunch." Easing away from her, he made short work of the condom and stood, six feet three inches of sculpted manhood.

Despite their recent activities, the sight had the power to dazzle her. She worked regularly with gorgeous movie stars. But she didn't get naked with them. She sat up and looked around for her clothes. They were scattered everywhere.

She untangled her panties from the wad of denim that was her jeans. "We should get dressed and eat lunch in the house."

"Let's not get dressed and eat right here."

"And then what?"

He winked. On Matt, a wink looked really good. "We'll have dessert."

"Are you by any chance putting off the moment when you walk into the house you bought?"

"I'm putting off the moment when you get dressed."

She got to her feet and stood facing him. "Flattering as that is, I can't shake the feeling that you're reluctant to go inside."

"After all the great things that happened out here, the inside of the house has lost its appeal."

"I get that, but you have to take a look sometime. Your family will expect to hear your thoughts on the place."

He shoved his fingers through his hair. "The idea of buying a ranch sight unseen sounded like a bold move back in LA, especially when Mom and Dad gave it their approval. But what if I hate it?"

"Then you renovate. Aren't you expecting to do that, anyway?"

"I am. Damon and Phil are all set to do the work. But I've never bought a house, let alone figured out what needed to be done with it."

"That's all the more reason to go inside. I don't pretend to know anything, either, but we can't talk about what we haven't seen. You have to start somewhere, get a general idea. Then you can bring Damon and Phil over and work out the specifics."

"Okay." He started pulling on his clothes. "That's another thing I have to decide. They're refusing to charge for labor. Just materials. I need to come up with a way to compensate them that doesn't involve giving them a check."

"How about tickets to the premiere?" She dressed quickly. She'd always been eager to see the house but Matt had been a powerful distraction.

His laughter had a bitter edge. "Yeah, right."

"Why not? That's a huge gift, especially if you fly them over."

"Is it? Months ago I set aside a bunch of money so I could treat anybody who wanted to be there. That was before this nastiness happened. Now I wonder if anyone will want to come or even if they should."

"Of course they'll want to come." Her heart broke for him, but this wouldn't be the only time he'd have to face ugliness. Hollywood was filled with gossip and innuendo. She spoke softly. "Matt, I know this is awful, but unfortunately it's part of the job."

"I know. I just didn't expect it first time out of the gate when my family is so excited for me. Eventually I'll get used to the way things are. They will, too. But I hate that it's spoiled something that was so shiny and new."

"Are you sure it has? I haven't been here long but I've already seen what the people in your family are made of. They won't let something like that keep them from celebrating your big moment. I'll bet nothing's spoiled in their minds. They love you."

Sighing, he picked up his hat and walked over to her. "You're right." He grimaced. "You'd think by now I'd believe in their loyalty." Handing over her glasses, he put on his hat. "Thanks for reminding me."

She hadn't meant to chide him but he'd taken it that way. Stepping closer, she touched his arm. "You've been sabotaged by someone you respected, someone you trusted. That would mess with anybody's head, but when you've dealt with something similar in the past, it has to be even more devastating."

He gave her a long look. "Yes, ma'am, that about sums it up." His gusty sigh of impatience was followed by a quick shake of his head. "But my past is no excuse. I've had the counseling. I spent more than ten years living at

Thunder Mountain Ranch. Everything that was broken has been fixed. At least, I hope to hell it has. Otherwise I have no business…"

"What?" The haunted expression in his eyes made her stomach churn.

"I have no business wanting to be with you."

"I want to be with you, too." Her grip tightened on his arm. "I love how I feel when we're together. And I'm not just talking about the sex."

"Neither am I. You're…you're magic." His jaw tensed. "But I'm starting to see a pattern. When I'm focused on you, everything's fine. Then I think about the injustice of it all, I lose my cool. That's not a good sign. Maybe I've been kidding myself. Maybe I'm still the same screwed-up kid I used to be."

She fought panic. "I'm sure you're not."

"Easy for you to say when you don't know what I was like. Any little thing would set me off. If somebody even suggested I'd made a mistake, or that I'd taken what wasn't mine, I lashed out."

"But you haven't lashed out."

"No, because I switched from lashing out to shutting down." He paused. "Does that ring a bell?"

She remembered the moment in her office when suddenly there was an invisible wall between them. "But you had a reason. I wasn't being—"

"Doesn't matter whether I had a reason. It's a bad coping mechanism and I'm supposed to be over it. I caused a problem for you by reacting that way. You had to make this whole damn trip because of my behavior."

"And I'm not the least bit sorry I flew out here! Are you?"

"No." His gaze softened. "I probably should be, but

I guess I'm pretty selfish. What we've had together has been incredible. I'm glad you ran after me."

"Me, too. And I wish you weren't making it sound like what we've had together is going away."

He cupped her face in both hands. "I could be a bad bet, Geena."

"Let me decide that, okay?"

"Not so easy." He brushed his thumbs over her cheeks. "You'd need a hell of a lot more background in order to make an informed decision."

"Then fill me in, catch me up."

"Don't know if that would work. Whenever I'm with you I'd rather kiss than tell."

"Okay by me." She sensed that the telling would be hard for him. "A lot of kissing, a little telling."

"Considering what happened today, I'd want to go way beyond kissing."

"So would I. I don't see a problem here."

"The sex is really good."

"Still no problem."

"It's likely to interfere with your judgment."

She met that comment with silence, unwilling to admit he had a point.

"See? You know I'm right. That means I should back off, at least until I know whether or not I have my act together."

"What if I don't feel like backing off? This is a two-person activity, you know."

"Are you threatening to seduce me?"

"I believe so, yes."

"Then you'll probably succeed and that won't get us anywhere."

"That's your opinion. I maintain it gets us all kinds of places, paradise being one. I like it there."

He held her gaze for several seconds and the struggle in his blue eyes was obvious.

"Tell you what," she said softly. "Let's go look at the house. We'll have lunch. We'll talk. And then...we'll see."

He took a shaky breath. "Okay."

Matt opened the front door and ushered Geena into the entry hall of his house. "This feels weird, like I'm trespassing."

"You'll get used to it the longer you're here." She walked straight ahead through an arch into the dim living room, where olive-green drapes covered a window. "Let's check out your view." She reached for the cord on the drapes and paused midmotion. "You should open them."

That made him smile. "This isn't the opening of a Broadway show. Go right ahead."

She pulled the cord and the drapes slowly parted to reveal a smudged picture window with a view of the Bighorns. "Bingo! I thought you might have a view of the mountains from this side of the house. The window's old as the hills, which is why there's so much dust on the floor. Look, you can see our footprints."

Sure enough, there were his large ones and her smaller ones. But not dainty. There was nothing fragile about Geena, and he needed to remember that. She'd survived living in Hollywood with an overbearing mother and she'd come out of that determined to do her own thing. She wouldn't allow him to selfishly mistreat her. That was a comforting thought.

Next they explored the side of the house that contained three kid-sized bedrooms and a small bathroom tiled in pink with green fixtures. The grout was stained and the faucets were corroded. Geena went in and barely had room to turn around. She glanced at Matt. "Any ideas?"

"A few. Most of them involve a sledgehammer."

She grinned at him. "See? Now you're getting the idea. Destroy the bathroom and start over. Enlarge it. Maybe knock out a wall between two of the bedrooms and put in another bath."

He nodded as he envisioned the changes. "That would make a big difference. Right now it seems cramped and dated." Worse yet, it reminded him of the kind of crummy places he'd lived in with his mother.

"Plus it would feel more like yours because you'd be putting your stamp on it."

"True. Okay, let's go see the other side. Maybe it's better."

It was. The kitchen appliances needed updating but he liked the black and white tile on the counters. Creating an arch between the kitchen and dining areas would open up that space. Finally they walked into the master bedroom and adjoining bath.

"This is nice." She turned in a slow circle in the middle of the bedroom. "You have views of the mountains through the west windows and a shade tree on the east side in case you want to sleep in."

"If I have horses I won't sleep in." But if he had Geena in bed with him, he'd have a conflict. Without a doubt he'd wake up wanting her.

"Right. Up at dawn, in bed before ten."

Yeah, something would be up at dawn, all right. The early bedtime appealed to him, though. With a woman like Geena, he might suggest they climb in around nine. "That schedule must seem really strange to you."

"It would in LA, but not here. This morning was gorgeous, and having animals depending on you is a great reason to swing your feet over the edge of the bed at dawn. It's a lot more exciting than fighting rush-hour traffic."

"Or catching the four-forty-five bus to the studio for a five o'clock makeup call."

"You could afford a car service now, Matt."

"I know." He gave her a crooked smile. "Old habits die hard and the bus feels familiar. I can afford a better apartment, too, but moving takes time and I haven't had much to spare. When I get back I'll look into hiring a car service, though. It would be more convenient, especially at that hour in the morning."

"I don't know how you can deal with those early calls. Either you or the makeup artists."

"It goes with the territory. I love acting, and if it can pay enough to maintain this ranch, I'll be a very lucky man." But the ranch wouldn't be much fun unless he had someone who'd enjoy it with him. He'd never craved solitude, maybe because he'd spent so much time alone in the first twelve years of his life.

The idea that he'd be living here by himself, or at best with a hired hand, hadn't occurred to him. He'd impulsively decided that a small ranch would be both a good investment and an excellent getaway. Yes, he could invite his family over, but he might end up spending most of his time at Thunder Mountain.

"Why the frown?"

Geena's question penetrated the fog of his increasingly negative thoughts. He looked up and his first instinct was to stonewall. Oh, boy. He took a deep breath and vowed to say what was on his mind. "I was thinking that buying this ranch could be a mistake."

She studied him for a moment. "Why?"

"For one thing, it's a lot of house for one person.

Or even for two, taking into account the hired hand. If Damon and Phil do the renovations you and I just talked about, it'll be a very nice house, too."

"Yes, it will."

"What if, after all that, I don't really want to be here?"

"Where would you want to be instead?"

He shrugged. "Over at Thunder Mountain. That's home."

"I know." Her gaze gentled. "I'll bet very few people walk into a vacant, unfurnished house, especially one that hasn't been lived in for months, and feel like it's home."

"I guess." Damn, but he wanted to hold her. She was sexy as hell but she also offered comfort. He wanted big helpings of both. He was about to take a step toward her when her stomach growled so loud it made her laugh.

"Sorry. I was about to say that if you just give it time, your feelings about the house might change."

"They might, but let's drop the subject and eat our lunch. We were supposed to bring it in here and we didn't. I'll go fetch it."

"Would you please bring my phone in, too?"

"Sure thing." As he headed out of the room, he vowed to get a grip on his emotions. Although her kindness and understanding made him want to wrap her in his arms, he really shouldn't do that until he had a better handle on what he was all about.

He retrieved her phone first and tucked it into his pocket. Then he pulled a lunch tote and two stainless steel water bottles out of Navarre's saddlebags and remembered that Rosie had put some chunks of carrot in there for both horses. So he fed them carrots and discussed his misgivings about continuing a relationship with Geena. Although they were great listeners, they didn't offer any solutions.

Even so, he felt more in control when he walked back into the house carrying lunch plus the blanket he hadn't bothered with earlier. Now it could serve as their table-cloth.

The minute he came through the door he heard a rhythmic clicking sound. When he realized what it was, he smiled. Sure enough, when he arrived at the double doors leading into the master bedroom, Geena was humming to herself while she danced around the perimeter of the room.

He leaned in the doorway, tipped back his hat and watched her. This house wouldn't be too big if she lived in it. Her sunny personality would fill every corner of every room.

She stopped when she noticed him.

"I thought you were supposed to keep dancing when you have an audience."

"That's the general rule, but in this case the audience is bringing lunch and I'm starving."

"I apologize." He handed over her phone. "We should have eaten a long time ago."

"Not if that meant skipping all the fun stuff." She glanced at the blanket.

"I brought this in so we'd have a tablecloth."

"Okay." She gave him a sunny smile. "If you don't mind, I'll check my messages while you set things up."

"Absolutely." He spread out the blanket.

"Well, that figures." She sighed.

"What?" He set the tote and water bottles on the blanket.

"One of my clients doesn't think we're getting him enough attention in the press. I thought I had it handled this morning, but apparently the reporter I contacted hasn't followed through."

"Do you need to follow up?"

"I'll have Larissa do it." She keyed in a reply to her assistant before sitting cross-legged on the floor next to the blanket. She laid her phone nearby. "Let's eat."

"Gotcha." He chose the opposite side, unzipped the tote and took out both sandwiches. "We have cookies for dessert."

"Yum."

"Mom never packs a lunch without putting cookies in it."

"Speaking of her, I've decided that if she'd enjoy seeing me dance, I'll do it. That's why I was practicing just now. Well, that and the fact that you were taking forever. I thought you'd be right back." She unwrapped her sandwich and bit into it. "Mmm."

That little moan had a predictable effect on his package. He took a deep breath and concentrated on unwrapping his sandwich. "Mom added some carrot pieces so Navarre and Isabeau could have a snack."

"Aw. That's adorable. If I'd known that I would have come out with you."

"I didn't remember until I opened the saddlebags. Anyway, I think dancing for her is a great idea. She'll love it."

"Good. Then I'm committed to making that happen." She finished another bite of her sandwich and put it down so she could open her water. "Just FYI, today is the first time I've danced in almost ten years."

"I never would have guessed."

"A professional would be able to tell in a minute. But I can feel it coming back, which is gratifying. I only mention the long layoff because you're the reason I felt like trying a few steps."

"Me?" He stared at her in surprise. "Why?"

"My mother's expectations sucked out the joy of dancing for me, which is why I quit the minute I had the guts to tell her I wasn't going to follow her plan for my future. Now do you understand?"

"No, not really. Unless you're saying because of me you've decided to go pro, after all."

"Not even close. I never want to become a professional dancer or singer. But being with you brings me joy. Dancing is my way of expressing that."

He stared at her. "No one's ever said something like that to me before."

"I thought you should know."

His throat tightened. "Thank you. That's...special."

"Yeah, it is." She smiled at him and picked up her sandwich. "Your turn to talk."

"About what?"

"Tell me about your mother."

Chapter Fourteen

Geena had expected the wall to come up between them, and it did. The process was both fascinating and sad. In the blink of an eye, Matt went from open and vulnerable to closed off and protected.

She ate her sandwich and waited to see if that would change. He continued to eat, too, and she wondered if they'd finish the meal in silence and ride back to the ranch without talking. She hadn't *asked* him to tell her about his mother. She'd practically ordered him to.

But fair was fair. He'd said she needed more background info, so she'd made up her mind not to discuss superficial things during their very private lunch. If she couldn't eat her sandwich off his six-pack abs, an image she'd cherished ever since they'd planned this trip, then she might as well search for a crack in the wall.

"Looking back on it, I realize she must have been an addict."

Geena had her water halfway to her mouth, but she put it down and glanced over at him. He wasn't looking at her, though. She doubted he was seeing anything in this room.

For a split second she wished she hadn't asked this of him. It was obviously very difficult. But if they were ever going to have a future, he had to start talking.

"She was always frazzled, distracted, not quite there." He heaved a sigh. "The day she didn't pick me up from school I thought she'd just forgotten. It had happened before." He paused to drink. His throat moved in several long swallows.

She longed to go to him and wrap an arm around his shoulders, but she didn't dare. That might stop the flow of words in favor of something that was easier for him— touch, physical pleasure. "Did she have a job?"

"She had jobs, or I guess she did. She was gone a lot. She got money somehow."

Geena immediately thought of prostitution but she wasn't about to say so. No doubt Matt had thought of it, too.

"There was never enough food in the house. She'd buy a loaf of bread and tell me not to touch it, so I wouldn't. Then half would be gone and she'd accuse me of eating it. She'd eaten it, but she'd been high and couldn't remember. Good thing I got free lunches at school, although in the summer…"

"You went hungry." Grief for that desperate little boy warred with white-hot anger directed at his mother.

"Yes, ma'am. But that wouldn't have been so bad if she'd only…" He turned toward her, and the pain reflected in his eyes took her breath away. "She didn't like me much."

"But she was an addict. She didn't even like herself, so how could she—"

"I know. The therapist said that, too. My mother wasn't capable of loving or even liking me. When she blamed me for everything and accused me of stuff I didn't do, that was her issue, not mine."

"Right."

"Damn it, Geena." He took off his hat and tunneled his fingers through his hair. "I've been through all this." Cramming his hat back on, he pushed himself to his feet. "I thought I was done with it."

She stood and watched as he began to pace like a caged animal. "I'm no therapist, but I can take a guess at what might be going on."

He turned to face her. "All right."

"You worked all this out and accepted that not everyone was like your birth mother. In fact, you haven't run into anyone remotely like her until you landed this movie role."

"I don't buy it. Briana's nothing like my mother. She's rich, successful, has a great husband. Maybe she drinks a little too much but she's not an addict. I'd have figured that out after working so closely with her."

"She may be more accomplished than your mother. Life has obviously given her more advantages. But from what you've told me, they have one big thing in common. They are completely focused on themselves. People they're in contact with are either an asset or a liability."

He gazed at her as if letting that sink in. "I was a liability to my mother."

"Absolutely. You required attention and resources and you were too young to bring anything to the table." Geena thought of her own mother. "If she'd operated in the environment where I grew up, she would have exploited your looks and talent. She would have made you a child star."

"So, you're saying I was lucky?"

"No." She hesitated to move any closer because this was important and shouldn't get tangled up in their physical attraction. "If you're lucky, then you have one, maybe even two parents who love you for yourself, not for the glory you bring to the family unit."

"Then I definitely was lucky because I ended up at Thunder Mountain. Mom and Dad are happy that I've made it this far, but they're happy for *me*, not because they'll get something out of it."

Dear Lord, she hadn't thought of that. Rosie and Herb couldn't ask Matt to help publicize their academy because he might think they were exploiting him. His link to them was pure, without commercial value.

She admired the hell out of the concept but it made her job that much harder. "You're really fortunate to have Rosie and Herb in your corner."

"And you."

"It's not the same. You pay me for my services."

"Do I pay you enough to suffer through that long layover in Denver?"

She smiled. "Point taken."

"Face it, Geena, this entire trip to Wyoming has been a bust. You can't justify it on a spreadsheet except under the heading Client Rescue Missions."

"I don't always think in terms of spreadsheets." She wasn't thinking of them now, for sure.

"That's one of the many things that makes you special." His gaze was warm at first, friendly and appreciative. Then gradually it darkened. The space between them seemed to shrink and the air grew still and hot.

The fire in his gaze made her burn with longing.

They'd talked this through, so what could be the harm in using that blanket for its original purpose?

She reached for him just as her phone chimed with a text from Larissa.

He backed up a step. "Your phone."

"I'll get it later."

"Get it now. See if it's important."

"Okay." With an impatient sigh, she turned and scooped up her phone. Then she let out a groan.

"What is it?"

"She can't get in touch with the reporter and the client is threatening to leave the agency if we don't make something happen in the next twenty-four hours. I'd let him leave but he's high profile and the agency's new enough that we really can't afford to lose him."

"Can you fix it?"

"Yes, but I'll need my laptop with my files to figure out where I can call in a favor."

"Then let's go back."

They talked about the renovations to the house on the return trip and she hoped he hadn't given up on keeping the place. No wonder he was worried about whether he'd made a mistake by buying it, though. After living for years with a critical woman who'd falsely accused him at every turn, he was sensitive to being judged for his personal decisions.

Fortunately for his career, he could take criticism directed at his acting ability. But Briana had attacked his character. With the unerring instincts of a bully, she'd hit him where he was most vulnerable.

When they arrived back at the barn, Cade happened to be coming out of it. "Hey, good timing. Just turn the reins over to me and scoot inside."

Matt objected because he obviously took his cowhand responsibilities to heart. It made Geena smile to watch the two brothers argue over who would take care of the horses.

Matt glanced at her. "You need to get going, though."

"I do, or I'd get in on this and help with the horses." She looked at Cade. "A client's throwing a hissy fit and I have to intervene."

"Will it take long?"

"I hope not. Why?"

Cade shoved back his hat. "Damon and Phil will be here in about an hour or so for our Skype powwow," he said.

"I should be finished by then."

"Great. You're gonna love this get-together. We've got us a Thunder Mountain think tank."

"Sounds good." She turned to Matt. "I'll be working in my room. Fingers crossed I can handle this quickly, but in case I'm still in there when people start arriving, would you please come get me?"

"Be glad to."

"See you both then." She gave Matt's arm a quick squeeze before starting for the house. On the way there she called Larisssa, who sounded a little panicky. "Don't worry," she said. "I'm at the ranch now and I'm on it."

Nearly an hour later, she shut down her laptop with a sigh. Disaster averted. She stood and stretched while she tried to decide whether to take her makeup case into the bathroom.

Matt's tap on her door answered that question. "Be right there." She quickly put on lipstick and ran a brush through her hair. Good enough. She hurried over to the door and opened it.

Matt stood there, eyebrows lifted. "Success?"

"Yes, thank God. He's being interviewed even as we speak and it'll run this weekend. He's thrilled and he's promised to recommend the agency to everyone he sees."

Matt laughed. "That's a little over the top."

"He won't do it, but at least he won't badmouth us, either, which is a relief."

"That's great news." He paused. "Ready for the next event? Damon and Phil are here."

"Okay. Good." Remembering her last meeting with Damon gave her an uneasy feeling in the pit of her stomach.

"I hope you don't blame him for the way he acted last night."

"Of course not. He was protecting you. In fact, I envy that. My mom kept me so overscheduled I didn't make lifelong friends who'd stick with me through thick and thin. My mom isn't the protective type, either, so I've been pretty much on my own."

"Well, you're not anymore."

She glanced at him in surprise. "What do you mean?"

"I've spent the last hour down at the barn grooming and feeding horses. Gave me some time to think. I don't know if I'm destined to be your lover, but I'll damned sure be your friend because you've been one hell of a friend to me. I'll always have your back, Geena." His gaze held hers. "Always."

"Thank you." She swallowed. "No one's...no one's ever said that they...anyway, thanks." She felt silly getting choked up about it, but he'd given her something she hadn't realized she'd been missing.

"You're welcome." His voice was low and tender. He likely hadn't expected such an emotional reaction from her, but his expression indicated that he understood why. "Let's go." He held out his hand.

"You want to walk in holding hands?"

"Yes. I want Damon and Phil to know that I…" He paused as if uncertain how to finish the thought given what he'd just said.

"That you have my back?"

He smiled. "Exactly."

"In that case, I'll be proud to hold your hand." She slid her fingers through his and the contact traveled through every part of her. She looked into his eyes. "Do you feel that?"

"If you're asking whether I get a buzz whenever I touch you, the answer is yes."

"Then maybe we shouldn't hold hands."

He gave her fingers a light squeeze. "Yes, we should." Then he grinned. "Unless you won't be able to control yourself."

Ah, how she'd missed that grin. "I can if you can."

"Then let's do this."

When they walked into the living room, everyone glanced in their direction and then, almost in unison, they looked down at Matt's hand linked with hers. It sent a powerful signal.

Rosie and Herb gazed at each other and smiled. Lexi gave Geena and Matt a subtle thumbs-up. Damon and Phil came straight over as if determined to set things right immediately. Phil carried their redheaded baby, who wore a shirt and shorts today.

"My apologies, ma'am." Damon touched his fingers to the brim of his hat. "I wasn't very hospitable last night."

"No apologies necessary." Geena absorbed the innate kindness in his brown eyes. "I showed up uninvited and you were protecting Matt."

"Yes, ma'am. But I was so focused on Matt's situation that I didn't even introduce Phil. I mean, Philomena."

Phil propped the baby on her hip and smiled at Geena. "Please call me Phil. Sophie's in a much better mood than she was last night, so this is a better meet and greet, anyway. Sophie, this is Geena Lysander, Uncle Matt's friend."

Geena gazed into the baby's wide blue eyes. "Hello, Sophie."

The little girl studied her with great interest as if trying to decide if this new person was someone she wanted to know. Apparently the answer was yes, because she held out both chubby arms and leaned in Geena's direction.

Phil laughed. "I guess you've made a friend, but you don't have to take her if you don't—"

"I'd love to hold her." She let go of Matt's hand and gathered the sweet-smelling baby into her arms. "But just to warn you, I don't know a thing about babies."

"That's what you said about horses, too." The affection in Matt's voice was unmistakable, which was both gratifying and embarrassing. Tipping back his hat, he beamed at her. "Turns out you're a natural."

"I'm guessing babies are harder to figure out than horses."

"Definitely," Phil said. "We didn't know anything about them, either. Rosie and Herb weren't baby savvy and neither was my stepmother. My dad ended up giving us all a crash course, since he was the one who'd raised me."

"Somehow we've managed, but sometimes it gets ugly." Damon grimaced. "Sophie loves her bath but she's slippery as an eel. Picture Phil soaked to the skin while she tries to keep the baby in the little bathtub. Meanwhile, I'm on the phone asking my father-in-law about diaper rash. Oh, and now Sophie's teething, which is a whole new circle of hell."

Matt clapped him on the shoulder. "Builds character."

"I'll remind you of that when you're getting up for feedings at two in the morning."

"Yeah, you would, too."

Geena doubted that anyone else had seen Matt's first reaction to Damon's teasing remark. The flash of anxiety in his blue eyes had been momentary, but she'd caught it. She could also guess why Damon's comment had hit a nerve. Matt didn't know if he was fit to be a husband, let alone a father.

Damon was too focused on his daughter to notice Matt's subtle mood swing. "She keeps us hopping." He paused to reach over and stroke her cheek with one finger. "But I love this little bugger."

During the conversation Sophie had been trying to grab Geena's glasses. Tucking the baby securely against her side, she managed to get them off and hand them to Matt. When she turned back to the little girl, Sophie grabbed a fistful of Geena's hair and yanked hard.

"*Ooh*, that smarts." She managed not to yell, or worse yet, swear.

"Uh-oh," Phil said. "Here, let me—"

"I've got it." Matt took Sophie's tiny fist and dropped mini kisses on it while he gently uncurled her small fingers. "Come see your uncle Matt," he crooned as he lifted her away from Geena's hair and into his arms. "See if you can pull my hair. Betcha can't."

Sophie must have sensed a challenge in his words, because she immediately knocked off his Stetson.

"That'll teach you, bro." Damon scooped it up and dusted it off. "But I'll have a talk with her about the sacred nature of a cowboy's hat. Otherwise she'll get herself in trouble messing with the Stetson."

"Ah, doesn't matter." Matt settled her in the crook of

his arm. Keeping his attention on the baby, he reached for Geena's glasses, which he'd hooked in the neck of his T-shirt, and gave them back to her while he continued his conversation with the little girl. "Like your daddy said, I dared you and you took me up on it. You've got game, Sophie. I predict a bright, shiny future's in store for you."

Those baby blues gazed at him as if mesmerized.

Sophie wasn't the only one caught in a net of adoration. Geena put on her glasses so she could more fully enjoy the sight of this tall, muscular cowboy sweet-talking an adorable baby. It was PR gold, but that wasn't why her breath caught and her pulse raced.

If someone had asked her five minutes ago to describe her perfect dream of the future, she wouldn't have been able to say what it was. But now she'd seen it.

Chapter Fifteen

"So, what about the house?" Damon looked at Matt and Geena as he asked the question. "Do you have a handle on what needs to be done?"

Geena decided to keep her mouth shut. She had no idea how Matt felt about the house at this point.

"I'm not sure I'm ready to answer that." Matt tickled Sophie's nose and she laughed.

"No worries," Phil said. "It might take several trips over there to think it through. If you want us to go with you next time, we'd be glad to."

Matt glanced up. "No rush. In fact, I'm wondering if I should have bought it in the first place."

Inwardly, Geena groaned. Matt was pulling back, re-evaluating his dreams. Not good.

"You are?" Damon's eyes widened in surprise. "Last night you were all about the ranch. You couldn't wait to go see it."

"I know, but I've been rethinking the concept. I'd hate for you and Phil to invest time in it when I'll only be able to enjoy the place sporadically. Besides, when I come back, I'll want to be here, not sitting over there by myself."

Both Damon and Phil looked confused, and Geena understood why. He'd walked in holding her hand, a clear indication they were a couple, and now he was talking about being alone in that house. His behavior wasn't making any sense but that wasn't surprising. His thoughts must be in turmoil.

He was saved from having to give them a better explanation when Ben and Molly Radcliffe arrived. Geena was delighted for the interruption. Matt was liable to dig himself into an even deeper hole if he kept talking about a future that was obviously unclear to him.

He introduced her to the newcomers and she liked them both on sight. Molly taught at the community college and had set up the academy curriculum. Ben was a saddle maker who offered academy students a chance to learn the basics of his trade. Molly talked Matt into giving up Sophie, and soon afterward, Cade announced the Skype call would begin in ten minutes.

Matt recaptured Geena's hand before they started toward Rosie and Herb's office. "I hope this works."

"I have a good feeling about it. It's your brothers, after all, and they only want the best for you."

"Good point." He took a deep breath and they walked down the hall.

She'd never peeked into the office, but she doubted it looked this way normally, with the computer connected to a large flat-screen and chairs grouped in two rows in front of it. Matt continued to hold her hand and Cade positioned them both front and center, with Rosie and Herb on one side, and Damon and Phil on the other.

"We're not key players," Damon said. "We don't need to be in front."

"Yeah, you do." Cade gestured to Sophie. "Everyone wants to see the baby. Before we address the problem, we need to let them go nuts over your kid." Then he turned to Geena. "I can introduce you first, though, since you're the guest—"

"Not necessary." She laughed. "It's an old Hollywood saying—never work with animals or kids. They'll upstage you every time. Let Sophie have her moment."

Cade nodded. "Good call. Has Matt briefed you on the folks we'll be talking to?"

"I know Finn's the Seattle brewer and Chelsea's the marketing guru he's in love with, and she likes to use interesting colors in her hair. But I have no info on the other couple you mentioned."

Matt glanced at the digital time on the screen. "We have a couple of minutes. I'll fill you in." He quickly told her about Ty Slater, his foster brother with the photographic memory who'd become a successful lawyer in Cheyenne, and Ty's wife, Whitney, a talented barista who managed a local coffee shop.

"It's time," Cade said. "Here's our agenda." He passed out sheets of paper to everyone.

"Agenda?" Damon laughed. "Seriously?"

"Seriously, bro. We need to stay on track. We'll have Sophie time for five minutes and then I'll ask Matt to introduce Geena and explain the situation. After that we'll throw it open for brainstorming."

"He gets this drill sergeant attitude from working with teenagers all day," Lexi said. "I've learned that once he's in this mode, it's best to just go along."

"I'm happy to." Geena was quickly becoming a Cade Gallagher fan. Obviously he'd taken on a leadership role and seemed to have a talent for it. He'd been right about providing some Sophie time. She was the first child born to a member of the brotherhood and she'd always occupy a place of honor because of that. She'd also have a passel of adoring uncles. The thought made Geena smile.

Sophie acted as if she already knew that she was a lucky girl. While everyone exclaimed over how cute she was and how big she'd grown, she waved her arms and bounced on Damon's lap as if welcoming the spotlight.

True to his word, Cade broke in on the baby party after five minutes to announce that they had to get on with the agenda. He took some more flak for his dedication to a timetable, but he stuck to his guns.

Matt introduced Geena and gave a brief overview of the PR issue they were working with. "Basically, what I'm looking for is a way to combat the negative publicity without creating a tabloid nightmare for anyone else, especially Mom and Dad."

Ty's wife, Whitney, a blonde with classic features, was the first to speak. "Like everybody here, I've been following the news about you ever since you got the part. I think it's wonderful that you landed it and I hate this for you, even though we don't really know each other."

"Thanks, Whitney. Rosie's told me so much about you, I feel like I know you."

"Same here." She smiled. "But I have a question. In all the stuff I've read or seen, no one's mentioned that you were a foster kid or that you lived in Wyoming, let alone at Thunder Mountain. Was that on purpose?"

Geena's breath caught. Apparently Whitney wasn't part of the inner circle and didn't realize that was a loaded question.

Matt wasted no time in answering her. "Yes, ma'am, it was definitely on purpose. I figured it was nobody's business. I didn't even tell Geena. And now I really can't bring it up even if I wanted to. Fans will think it's a bid for sympathy."

"I cherish my privacy, too." Ty put his arm around his wife. "Whitney will testify to that. But when I ended up on the academy's promo calendar two years ago, my story was out there for all to see. That made me *really* uncomfortable. But since then a lot of foster kids have told me they were inspired because I overcame the odds."

"Same here," Damon said. "I was asked to give a talk at the high school on that very subject. I had a couple of emails after that from kids who said they weren't going to think of themselves as victims anymore."

Matt nodded. "I can understand why talking to you would help them. I'll admit I never considered that angle. I will from now on."

"But you're right about bringing the info to light now." Chelsea tucked her hair, streaked with various shades of green, behind her ears. "So, Geena, what are your thoughts? I'm sure you've been thinking about how to fix things."

"I have."

Chelsea's expression grew animated. "Great! What-cha got?"

Geena hesitated. Was there any point in laying out a plan that Matt would hate? But, judging from her conversation with Cade earlier today, everyone else might go for it. She could be pitting him against his family.

"This is a brainstorming session." From his position in the second row, Cade reached over and laid a hand on her shoulder. "We need to hear all the ideas."

She turned to Matt. "You won't care for it."

His gaze was steady. "Like Cade said, anything goes in a brainstorming session."

Technically that was true, but he could consider her suggestion a betrayal, especially if the others jumped on board and he became the one dissenting voice.

Matt knew exactly why he'd agreed to this Skype session. Cade had invoked the Thunder Mountain Brotherhood code. In high school Matt had stood by his brothers whenever some guy with spaghetti for brains decided to make fun of the foster boys who lived at Thunder Mountain. Apparently their loyalty to each other bothered certain types of people, mostly bullies.

Now Matt was the one being threatened by a bully and his brothers were here to support him and make sure he didn't back down. He appreciated their support, but he trembled to think what kind of scheme Geena had dreamed up. She'd forewarned him that he wouldn't like it and so chances were good he'd hate it.

But he couldn't ask Geena to withhold her idea. Ultimately she couldn't force it on him, anyway. He was still the client.

"Okay, here goes." Geena sat up a little straighter. "What if Thunder Mountain Academy makes a promotional video during this break between semesters, and the story we put out is that Matt flew here specifically so he could be in it?"

Matt groaned. "That's—"

"Brilliant!" Chelsea said. "I love it! Instead of looking as if you ran away to dodge bad publicity, we show that leaving LA had nothing to do with that."

"That's the idea." Geena gripped his hand tighter.

"Matt, this could really work." Chelsea's expression was animated. "Fans will love that you're donating time to promote your family's enterprise. Make the video tomorrow and finish it by sundown. The video is released along with press about it, providing great publicity for the academy and wholesome PR for you. It's genius."

"Except making that video with me in it will destroy Mom and Dad's privacy." Letting go of Geena's hand for the first time since they'd sat down, Matt turned to them. "This place is special. You don't want reporters knocking on your door, asking invasive questions. You don't want—"

"Son." Rosie put her hand on his arm and looked into his eyes. "I'm not sure where you got this notion that privacy is important to us. We used to have up to twelve boys at a time living on this ranch, but after we retired we had more privacy than you could shake a stick at. We *hated* it."

"Yeah, we did," said Herb. "We've never worried about opening our home to others. When we ran a foster care facility we had to have the premises inspected regularly. After we got a reputation in the state for our work with kids, we were featured several times on TV."

"You were? I don't remember that."

"They interviewed us when you were all in school. Identifying any of you would have been an invasion of privacy because you were underage." Herb's voice gentled. "But now that we're running the academy, we're actively seeking publicity, so making a video is a great idea. But you don't have to be in it if that makes you uncomfortable."

"But would you even want my name attached to the academy with all the negative stuff that's been said about me this week?"

Rosie squeezed his hand. "We're not worried about

that. But we'd never want to exploit your fame for our benefit. That's not—"

"Wait. You're worried about *using me*?"

She nodded.

"We've all worried about that," Damon said. "Lots of times when people get famous their relatives take advantage. That's not who we are."

Sophie picked that moment to start fussing and Damon stood. "Sorry, everybody. I think Sophie's done with this Skype thing."

"Yep, it's dinnertime for her." Phil got up, too. "Hate to run. Great seeing you guys!"

Everyone on the screen called out goodbyes, and the baby was distracted by that and stopped fussing long enough for Damon and Phil to make a more leisurely exit. They'd all be seeing each other in August for Cade and Lexi's wedding, and while that event was being discussed, Matt had a chance to sort through what he'd just been told. Gradually the truth sank in, and as it did, he felt lower than a snake's belly.

He hadn't been protecting his family. He'd been protecting himself and his vision of retreating from the craziness of LA to the idyllic privacy of his home at Thunder Mountain. Talk about selfish.

If he'd been thinking about his folks instead of himself, he would have realized that the academy was a business like any other. Geena had tried to tell him he could help out when she'd mentioned the girls who'd stayed in the cabin they'd been cleaning earlier. He hadn't listened.

Oh, his motives had seemed so noble, but now they looked totally self-serving. He needed to get over himself and concentrate on being an asset to his parents' business. Teenagers liked movie stars. He'd idolized his share when he'd been that age. He hadn't cared if they got in a little trouble now and then. It made them human.

But he hadn't been willing to admit how much he could contribute to the cause because he'd been focused on his need for privacy. And why was that? A cold chill ran down his spine as the answer came to him. His mother. He could hide from her in LA, no problem. Not here.

His gut told him she wasn't that far away. She'd probably stayed in Wyoming all these years, where she knew the public assistance programs inside out and the cost of living was reasonable. If he made the video tomorrow and left town before it was released, he likely wouldn't have to deal with her.

But Rosie and Herb might. They could handle her, of course, but they shouldn't have to. She'd been nasty fifteen years ago and he doubted she'd changed. According to what he'd learned about her personality type, she was probably worse.

"Matt."

He turned to look at Geena. "It's okay." He hated seeing the anxiety in her green eyes, especially knowing he'd been the one who'd caused her to worry. "I'll do the video. Even more important, I want to."

She sighed and her shoulders relaxed. "Okay. That's good."

"But just so you know, my birth mother could see the video and contact the ranch looking for me. I'll alert Rosie and Herb."

"I'm sure they'll run interference for you."

"That's just it. I don't want them to. I'll stay an extra two days after the video goes live to give her plenty of time to make the call. If she does, I'll take it and invite her to the ranch."

Chapter Sixteen

Geena had no time to respond to that startling announcement because Sophie grew restless again and Damon and Phil left for real. That turned everyone's attention back to Matt and the prospect of a video being made within the next twenty-four hours.

"I'm absolutely doing it," he said. "Assuming it's even possible to get something like that together in a hurry."

"We mostly need a videographer." Geena turned in her seat to look at Cade, Lexi, Molly and Ben. "Any ideas?"

"Yes." Molly fairly crackled with energy. "One of the instructors at the community college, Drew Martinelli, would be perfect if she hasn't left on vacation yet." She pulled her phone out of her purse. "I'll text her now."

Lexi jumped on the idea. "This is serendipity. Cade and I need someone to video our wedding, so if she works out for this, maybe we could hire her for August."

"She'd be great." Molly typed quickly. "I just hope she's still in town."

"We need to have a potential script," Chelsea said from the screen. "Finn has to head back to O'Roarke's but I can stay on the call if you need my help."

"Yes, please." Geena turned to give her a quick smile.

"Whitney and I have to sign off, too," Ty said. "We're having dinner with her folks. But if you need anything, holler, and text or email us when it's up."

"Will do." Cade glanced at the screen. "Thanks for being here, both of you. See you in August. Lexi and I are expecting a really big present."

Ty laughed. "We're getting you a very expensive kitchen gadget, bro, now that you're such a gourmet cook."

"Can't wait." Cade grinned. "Hey, thanks for being here." Cade walked over to the computer. "So, it's Chelsea and Geena on this project so far. Who else is volunteering to work out a script?"

"I will," Rosie said.

"I'll help, too," Lexi said. "I've commissioned a few videos of my riding clinics, so I know a little about the process."

Geena decided somebody needed to take charge of the project and she was the logical one. "If we have Chelsea, Rosie, Lexi and me, that should be enough."

"And me," Matt said. "I've had some experience with scripts."

She gazed at him. "Yes, you have, and thanks for the offer."

"It's the least I can do."

His smile tugged at her heart, but now wasn't the time for a private conversation about how he was handling this turn of events.

"There's Drew." Molly grabbed her phone and glanced at the incoming text. "She's available all day tomorrow."

"Excellent." Geena took that as a positive sign that the video was meant to be. "I know this is a lot to ask, but if she can show up before dawn, she'll get some amazing footage."

"Let me see what she says." Molly typed in the request and waited. "Yes! In fact, she'd thought of that herself. She'll be here before five tomorrow morning."

"Good. Thank you, Molly. That's huge."

"Call if you need anything else." Molly left with Ben.

"Looks as if you have everything under control," Cade said. "I leave the project in your capable hands." He glanced at Lexi. "See you at home."

"You will. Fabulous job, cowboy."

"Thanks." He touched the brim of his hat and left with Herb.

"Okay, then," Chelsea said. "Where do we start?"

Geena knew where that should be. She just didn't think the man sitting beside her would go for it. "The video will publicize the academy, but let's get real. Matt's our biggest draw. We should start the video with him." She glanced in his direction. "Does that work for you?"

He met her gaze with surprising calmness. "Yes, it does. I should probably narrate the thing. Since we have the videographer committed to arriving before dawn, the script should begin with an exterior shot as the sun's coming up. Then pan to the barn, tight focus on the barn door and head inside to where I'm doing something."

"Something manly," Chelsea said, as computer keys clicked. "Like pitching clean hay into a stall. Keep talking. I'm writing all this down."

"Are the horses out or in?" Lexi moved up to the front row and sat next to Geena.

"Out in the pasture," Geena said. "More dramatic.

It would be great if we could get them to race around a little."

"I have an idea." Matt leaned forward as if he actually might be enjoying the process. "Put Cade out with the horses. Have him grab a handful of mane and swing up bareback on Hematite. That's always a crowd pleaser. Once he gets Hematite moving, Linus will follow and the others might, too."

"I can just picture it." Rosie's face glowed. "It'll be wonderful. Oh, I know what else we need in this video! We could use some roof repair on Cabin Three. Let's get Damon up there and film him doing it."

"Nice." Chelsea kept typing. "Stetson, snug T-shirt, jeans and a tool belt. Damon rocks that look."

"Before we go any further, I want to say something else." Rosie looked around at the group. "Phil deserves to be up on that roof as much as Damon. Lexi, you have every right to ride bareback along with Cade. I don't mean to be sexist, but—"

"The video needs to be about the brotherhood," Lexi said. "I figured that out right away. We know what we want to accomplish and putting great-looking cowboys in each shot is the way to go."

Geena nodded. "It is. We'll want a scene with Rosie and Herb, but other than that, it's all about the Thunder Mountain Brotherhood." Geena glanced over at Matt. "Are you comfortable talking about that connection?"

"You bet. Until Ty mentioned it, I never considered that our story might help other foster kids. And I should have. I wish that I'd—"

"Don't be too hard on yourself," Geena said. "We've all known celebrities who milked their tragic past to get attention. You didn't want to be that person."

He gave her a distracted smile. "Thanks."

"That's what will be so great about this video," Chelsea said. "We have a talented actor narrating it. I predict this thing will go viral in no time."

"Hallelujah!" Rosie threw both hands in the air. "I've always wanted a viral video!"

"Me, too." Chelsea said. "We need to nail down the rest of the scenes so we can turn Matt and Geena loose on the dialogue. I figure you two are the movie people, so you're the logical ones to handle it."

Matt nodded. "No problem."

After everyone agreed on the order of scenes, Chelsea emailed her notes to Geena and signed off.

Lexi glanced at Geena and Matt. "I'll leave you to it. Writing dialogue is so not my area."

"Not mine, either," Rosie said. "I'll rustle up your dinner and bring it in here so you can keep working."

After Rosie walked out the door, Geena gazed at Matt. She didn't have the words to express her admiration or her frustration. The two emotions were hopelessly tangled up in her mind, so instead of saying anything, she grabbed him and kissed him with enough force to knock off his hat.

He obviously wasn't expecting it and he froze.

Lifting her mouth a fraction of an inch, she took a quick breath. "Steam up my glasses, damn it. You know you want to."

With a groan, he pulled her close and his mouth came down on hers.

Oh, yes. She surrendered completely to the pleasure of kissing Matt. This was what he should be doing instead of worrying about whether he was the right guy for her. How could he doubt it when these moments of shared passion were so amazing?

Breathing unevenly, he pulled back. "We have to stop."

"I know. Rosie will—"

"Be here any minute." And he recaptured her mouth.

So sweet. So hot. She couldn't imagine living without his kiss.

He lifted his head again. "Enough." Blowing out a breath, he released her and stood. "I told myself I wouldn't do this."

"You didn't. I did." She gulped for air. "Not your fault."

"I could have said no." He located his hat on the floor and picked it up.

She smiled as she took off her glasses and polished them on her shirt. "I don't think so. I'm irresistible."

"Yes, ma'am, you sure as hell are." He ran his fingers through his hair and took a deep breath. "Before Rosie comes back, I need to clarify something I said earlier. Although I'm staying a couple more days, I don't expect you to."

"If you're staying, I'm staying."

He shook his head. "Let me put it another way. I'd rather you didn't."

Wow, that hurt. She was prepared to stick by him during a difficult time and he wanted her gone. She struggled to regain her composure. "Assuming your birth mother actually shows up, I won't be shocked by her, if that's what you're worried about. I have a fair idea of what to expect."

"How can you, when I don't? She was pretty messed up the last time I saw her. If she decides to come here, there's no telling what she'll be like. You don't need to experience that."

"What if—" She paused to clear her throat. "What if I want to?"

"Geena, I'm asking you to head back to LA." He put on his hat and tugged down the brim. "Please."

"Why?"

His voice was tight. "Maybe I should let you stay so you can see where I came from."

She clutched her denim-clad knees to keep her hands from shaking. "I know where you came from and it doesn't matter. No, I take that back. It does matter. Knowing your background makes me admire you that much more."

"Admire me? You've got to be kidding."

"Of course I admire you! You could have let your past define you. Instead, you set an ambitious goal and achieved it."

"All because my past *does* define me. Haven't you been paying attention? I'm as selfish as my mother!"

She gasped. "You are not! How can you say such a thing?"

"Look at the evidence." His bitter tone sent a chill through her. "I insisted that Rosie and Herb needed privacy when I really wanted privacy for *me*. I rejected your idea that I could help publicize the academy because it would louse up my precious retreat plans. It's always been about my needs, not theirs."

She had trouble breathing, but she forced the words out as best she could. "Matt, it happens to everyone. We think we're doing something noble and it turns out our motives were self-serving. But you figured it out and now you're doing the right thing."

"Or maybe I see a way to save my own hide and I'm taking it."

"No! You see a way to set everything right. You benefit and the academy benefits. It's a win–win!"

"Even if it turns out that way, and I hope it does,

that doesn't change anything. I clearly have the ability to block out everything except what I want. I lived with that woman for twelve years. I've kidded myself that I escaped who and what she was, but—"

"I guarantee that you have."

His gaze was shuttered. Not completely closed, yet, but it wouldn't take much for the wall to come up. "I wish I could believe that, but I can't."

"Then why wait for your mother? What's in it for you? If she does come here, I doubt it will be pleasant. You could leave before the video release and lock her out of your life forever. You could surround yourself with enough security that she'd never get through."

He looked as if he wanted to pace but the room was cluttered with furniture. He turned a chair backward and straddled it so he was facing her. "Once again, selfish motives. I told myself I had to stay and protect Rosie and Herb from having to deal with her, but that's not the real reason."

"Why can't it be one of the reasons? I'm sure they'd appreciate having you here if she comes calling."

"They probably would, but my main reason for staying has nothing to do with them. I want to find out if there's any trace of regret for what she did. But more than that, I need to know if I'll look at her and see myself."

"There's bound to be some resemblance, Matt. She gave birth to you."

"That's not what I mean."

"I know. I've done the same with my mother. I like to think I've taken after my father." Then she wished she hadn't said it. Matt couldn't use that strategy.

"Doesn't apply." His expression gave nothing away. The wall had come up.

"Dinner's served!" Rosie came bustling in with Herb

right behind her. Both were carrying trays. Matt jumped up immediately to help and Geena followed suit.

As they cleared a place on the desk to set the plates of food and bottles of O'Roarke's Pale Ale, Rosie's and Herb's forced cheer suggested that they'd heard at least part of the argument. The concern in Rosie's eyes as she glanced at Matt confirmed it.

Geena considered asking them to stay so they could bring the issue out in the open. But she might make the situation worse and she was a guest who'd been here less than forty-eight hours. Forcing an intervention seemed disrespectful.

After they left, she looked at Matt. "Are you going to be able to work on dialogue with me?"

"Yes. It needs to be done."

Of course he'd be able to do it. He was a professional. So was she. "I'll get my computer."

Chapter Seventeen

Matt knew he was behaving like a jerk and yet he couldn't stop himself, which was proof that he wasn't the guy for Geena. It was now clear as a bell to him, so he wished she'd accept it, too. The sooner she left town, the better, but everyone would expect her to stay until the video was finished and she would insist on it out of professional pride.

That meant she couldn't leave until the day after tomorrow, because of limited flights out of Sheridan. Which left a hell of a lot of hours to endure, especially when every time he looked at her he longed to pull her into his arms and kiss those full lips. More proof that he was a selfish bastard.

She reappeared with her laptop and he fought the urge to take it out of her hands and apologize for every terrible thing he'd said. He'd told her to leave when he desperately needed her to stay. He'd said they were wrong for each other when every time he held her it felt so right he wanted to shout for joy.

But that was his selfish side talking, the part he'd inherited from his screwed-up, narcissistic mother. For Geena's sake, he couldn't listen to that voice. He had to continue to push her away until she finally got the message.

They plunged into the dialogue project like the pros they were. They didn't eat much but they drank all the beer. In Matt's current frame of mind, another couple of bottles would have been welcome. But he wasn't going back to the kitchen to get them. Rosie would waylay him, for sure. He'd seen the look on her face when she'd brought the food. She knew something wasn't right.

Writing the dialogue under these circumstances was a tough slog, but he and Geena pulled it off. She emailed the finished product to Drew, who'd use it to plan the sequence of shots.

At last she closed her laptop and stood. "That does it."

He got to his feet, too. "Yes, ma'am, it does."

Irritation flashed in her green eyes. "If you're such a heinous person, why bother with the gentlemanly behavior?"

"Maybe it gets me what I want."

Her jaw tightened. "Are you implying that you used that *yes, ma'am* routine to get me out of my clothes?"

He could tell she was tired and pushed to the limit. The more obnoxious he was, the quicker she'd dump his sorry ass. "It worked, didn't it?"

She slapped him so hard it brought tears to his eyes. Good. He deserved it.

"This is not who you are." Her voice was choked with fury. "If you were really that rotten, Rosie and Herb wouldn't love you."

"They see what they want to see."

She growled in frustration and started out of the room. "I'll be back for the dishes. I'm sure Rosie and Herb have gone to bed by now and we need to clean up our mess."

"Don't worry about the dishes. I'll take care of them."

"Okay, Great." She paused in the doorway and turned around. "Feel free to sleep in your room tonight. My door will be locked, so no temptation there."

"Thanks for the thought, but I'll sleep in the barn again."

"Why do that? You and I are so done."

"That's not what your eyes say." He'd keep it up until she hated him.

"I don't give a damn what my eyes say. My mouth says we are *done*, cowboy. I'm locking my door."

"In that case, I probably should warn you there's something else I learned from my worthless mother."

"What?"

"I can pick locks."

"Then I should warn you of something I learned from my mother."

"Oh?"

"How to deliver a well-placed knee to the groin."

In spite of everything, that made him smile, but he ducked his head so she wouldn't see. Dear God, how he loved her. Then he went very still as the insight played in a slow motion loop in his head. *He loved her?* Well, yeah, of course he did. Otherwise he wouldn't be so determined to sabotage any feelings she'd developed for him.

He kept his head down until he heard her huff of anger and her retreating footsteps. Hiding his smile was about maintaining a consistent message. Hiding his love was about survival.

* * *

Anger fueled an adrenaline rush that carried Geena through her bedtime routine as she took a shower, and washed and dried her hair. Then she lay in the dark, eyes open, and prayed for him to come through the door. She hadn't locked it, had never intended to. Not that they would make love in this room, not with Rosie and Herb sleeping nearby.

But if he'd come to her and taken back all those mean things he'd said, they could escape to the barn and put things right between them. She longed to rewind the clock to this morning when he'd been so wild for her he'd risked being discovered by Lexi and Cade, or this afternoon when they'd made sweet love on a cool patch of green grass.

This evening, with the help of his folks, and his brothers and their wives, they'd created a potential solution to his PR disaster, but at what cost? He'd begun to doubt himself before the Skype call, and the revelations from that phone meeting had left him shattered. Another person might reluctantly acknowledge their self-serving behavior and vow to do better. Not Matt. He was drowning in the shame of thinking he was just like his mother.

She thought of her own mother, who had, in fact, taught her the knee-to-groin move. Although Geena liked to believe she took after her late father, she had many of her mother's traits, including fierce determination, which could easily become stubbornness.

Her mom had force-marched her through years of performance training, which had taught her self-respect and discipline. Her mom had been absent a lot, but she'd never completely abandoned the field. Geena had become self-reliant out of necessity, but that wasn't a bad quality.

Without the upbringing her mother had provided, she might not have had the guts to follow Matt to Sheridan. She definitely wouldn't have had the discipline to knock out a video script despite the tension that had ricocheted around the room the entire time. And the person she'd become would not lie staring at the ceiling until dawn, either.

Climbing out of bed, she put on her glasses. Then she located the boots Rosie had loaned her and the flashlight tucked in the bedside table drawer in case of a power outage. Once again she'd play the role of uninvited guest. He might turn her away. In fact, he probably would. But she had to try.

Rosie and Herb hadn't bothered to lock up, so she was able to slip out easily while carrying her boots and flashlight. Locked doors seemed to be a rarity in the country, which made her earlier comment to Matt all the more ludicrous. She wasn't sure her bedroom door even had a lock.

Cool air greeted her as she stepped out on the porch and sat in one of the Adirondack chairs to put on her boots. The ranch looked different at night, a little bit alien with only the dusk-to-dawn lights illuminating the circular drive and the barn several yards away. She descended the steps. The crunch of her boots on the gravel drive seemed unnaturally loud in the stillness. When a cricket chirped in the bushes beside the porch she jumped.

Placing a hand over her racing heart, she paused to take several deep breaths. She could do this. The barn wasn't that far away. She started out, putting her feet down carefully so her boots on the gravel wouldn't sound so much like somebody chewing potato chips.

No one was out here, so it might not matter, but she didn't want to attract attention from…anything. Belatedly she remembered that Wyoming was filled with wildlife. She'd heard that making a lot of noise would frighten animals away, but she wasn't sure that was true of really big creatures like bears.

Okay, now she was scaring herself. Time to calm the heck down. Once she'd passed outside the glow of the first yard light, she lifted her head to look at the stars. *Oh, my.* They covered the navy-blue sky like spilled sugar. She'd never seen so many.

Then she heard something. Glancing wildly around, she saw a shadow near the barn door. A pretty big shadow, like a bear on its hind legs would make. She tried to yell but only managed a tiny squeak. She was so stupid to come outside by herself! And now a bear would eat her and she'd never get to tell Matt that she—

"Geena?" Matt stepped into the light hanging over the barn as his long strides quickly eliminated the distance between them. "What in God's name are you doing out here?"

"I—I…wh-what are *you* doing out h-here?" Her teeth chattered as relief washed through her, leaving her weak and trembling. "I thought y-you were a b-bear!"

"Ah, Geena." He gathered her close and rested his cheek on the top of her head as he rocked her gently back and forth. "What am I going to do with you?"

"Is th-that a rhetorical question or d-do you want an answer? Because I c-can give you some ideas if you n-need any." She held on to his solid warmth and gradually the quivery feeling subsided.

His body started to shake and eventually she realized he was laughing. He'd muffled the sound in her hair, which was probably a good idea because maybe a bear really was lurking nearby. She'd seen grizzlies on

TV. Two people, even one built like Matt, were no match for a grizzly.

Even so, she felt a thousand percent safer in his arms than she had walking through the dark alone.

Finally he cleared his throat and gazed down at her. "What sort of ideas would you like to offer me?"

"Could we discuss this in the barn? I'm worried about bears."

"There aren't any bears around."

"How do you know?"

"The horses would get agitated."

"Oh. Well, good, but I'd still like to have this conversation inside, if you don't mind."

"Of course I mind." But as he said it, he drew her closer, which revealed that a certain significant part of him didn't mind at all. "I came down here to get away from you, and then you show up in your Captain America shirt and your boots, and you must have washed your hair because it smells amazing."

"I did wash it." She began to quiver for a different reason altogether. "And I admit I did that for you. I thought maybe you'd come to my room and we could...talk."

"Talk. Right." He rubbed her back, moving gradually lower until he cupped her bottom and pulled her in tight. "I thought you were planning to lock your door."

Her body warmed as his fingers flexed, creating an arousing massage. "Does it even have a lock?"

"No." And he started laughing again. "We'd better head for the barn before this gets any hotter and we wake up the folks. In the summer they like to sleep with their windows open." Looping an arm around her shoulders, he guided her toward the big double doors. "I should be walking you back to the house, but I can't seem to make myself do that."

"I'm glad. I really…the way we left things was…"

"It was awful. That's why I was outside, just looking up at the stars and thinking. I kept wondering if I should go back to the house and at least apologize, but then I knew you'd be in bed wearing that sleep shirt and the inevitable would happen."

"It wouldn't have."

"You would have rejected me?"

"No, I would have insisted we come down here, away from the house."

He looked at her and smiled. "You knock me out, you know that?"

"Yes, because you knock me out, too, which is why—"

"Nothing's changed. We'll go into the barn and make love because I can't stand not to, but after that…"

"I have an idea. Let's not think about what happens after that."

He took a deep breath. "Good thinking." He ushered her into the dim interior, lit only by small lights along the aisle between the stalls. "Wait here." He ducked into a room just inside the barn door.

She breathed in the scent of hay, horses and oiled leather while she listened to various snorts and soft groans, the clunk of a hoof against a floorboard and the rustle of straw. She loved being here because this was Matt's territory, one he could share with her if only he would. The possibility of that didn't seem very high at the moment.

But she'd suggested to him that they should forget about both the past and future, and concentrate on the present. Good advice. She ought to take it.

He reappeared, a blanket under his arm. "This way." Grasping her hand, he led her down the wooden aisle to an empty stall.

The door was open, and now that her eyes had adjusted, she could make out mounds of straw inside. "Is this where you slept last night?"

"Yes, ma'am." He unfolded the blanket and laid it out on the straw.

"Can you do something with these?" She handed her glasses to him.

"We'll hook them over the stall door latch." He made sure they were secure, draping his hat over them. "That should do it." He turned to her, his hands on his hips. Then he sighed. "You know what? This is nuts. I'm taking you back to the house. Making love again will only—"

"Don't you dare back out now, cowboy." Launching herself at him, she nearly knocked him over.

He staggered when he caught her but he managed to keep them upright. "Geena, come on. This is crazy."

"Shut up and kiss me." She grabbed him around the neck and pulled his head down. If she could get him in a lip-lock, he'd be toast.

"It's a mistake."

"We're doing it anyway."

He groaned. "Looks like it." And when his mouth found hers, there was no doubt. He kissed her with the hunger of a man barely in control. He broke away only long enough to pull the sleep shirt over her head and toss it down. Then he lowered her to the blanket and began tasting every inch of her.

Gasping, she writhed on the blanket. "My...boots."

"I'm leaving 'em." He kissed his way from her breasts to her navel. "I've never made love to a woman wearing boots." He planted soft kisses along her trembling thighs. "I'm guessing you've never made love to a man while wearing them, either."

She moaned. "Good guess."

"I'm all wrong for you." He blew gently on her damp curls. "But I'm selfish enough to want you to remember me." And he settled into the most intimate kiss of all.

She'd remember him, all right, whether she kept the boots on or took them off. A woman didn't easily forget a man who gave her more pleasure than she'd ever dreamed possible. Her climax arrived with such force that she pressed the back of her hand to her mouth to keep from yelling.

After bestowing a few more tender kisses in strategic places, he moved away and began stripping off his clothes. As she lay on the soft blanket, sprawled in reckless abandon, she wished they had more light because he was the most beautiful man she'd ever seen and this might be the last…no, she wouldn't think about that. Worrying about the future robbed her of precious time with him tonight.

Her body hummed with anticipation. Before long they'd once again experience that magic connection and they'd share the joy of…wait a minute. He hadn't expected her to walk down here. "Matt, do you have a condom?"

"Yes, ma'am." His breathing was a little ragged.

"How could you, when you weren't expecting me?"

"Pure luck." Foil crinkled. "I left the rest of the box hidden in the tack room this morning. After our conversation today, I didn't figure I'd have a use for them." He lowered himself to the blanket, propped himself on his outstretched arms and settled between her thighs. "You changed my mind." His face was in shadow as he leaned down and brushed his mouth over hers.

"I'm encouraged that I can do that." She ran her hands up his muscular chest and savored the tactile thrill of springy hair beneath her palms.

"Don't be encouraged. It's temporary." He nibbled on her lower lip.

"Oh, Matt, I wish—"

"You're thinking about the future. You told me not to."

"I know."

"Don't think, just…feel." He slid in smoothly, effortlessly.

Sighing, she lifted her hips to bring him closer. "Like that?"

Muttering a soft oath, he held very still. "Yes, ma'am."

"It does work."

"What?" His voice sounded strained.

"Those cowboy manners." She explored the manly terrain of his broad shoulders. "To get me naked."

"That was a stupid thing to say. I didn't mean it."

"I know." She stroked lower and pushed her fingertips into his impressive back muscles.

He sucked in a breath. "I wanted you to be mad at me."

"I was, but I'm sorry I slapped you."

"I deserved it." He feathered a kiss over her lips. "But right this second, I have a problem."

"What?"

"I desperately want to start moving, but I don't have much control. I'm liable to get a little crazy. Can you handle that?"

Her heartbeat kicked into high gear. "Uh-huh."

"Then hang on."

He wasn't kidding. It was the wildest few minutes of her life, and the most thrilling, too. His intensity triggered an orgasm before she expected it, but he kept going, urging her on as he stroked faster, and faster yet.

"Again." He changed the angle and she gasped, on the brink of a second climax.

He bore down and she came. Jaw clenched, he stifled

a deep groan as he surrendered to his own release. He shuddered in the grip of his orgasm then he slowly lowered his body and allowed it to rest lightly against hers.

She stroked his sweaty back. "Relax," she crooned. "Let go."

At last he did, nestling his body against hers. The tension slowly drained away and she thought he might be asleep, or at least dozing.

She might never have a better chance to say what was in her heart. "I love you," she murmured softly.

He didn't stir. He probably was asleep, and that was okay. She'd needed to say it and now she had.

Chapter Eighteen

After Geena drifted off to sleep, Matt eased away from her, took care of the condom and set the alarm on his phone. Then he gathered her into his arms and held her as he savored the words she'd spoken. He'd never forget that she'd said them, even though he wouldn't be building dreams based on her words of love.

She might believe what she'd said, but she'd glossed over his failings because she was generous that way. Incredible sex had a way of affecting a person's judgment. It certainly had affected his. Until the Skype call he'd thought he might have a future with her.

But he could see the situation clearly now, even if she couldn't. He was still too mired in his toxic past to be with anyone, and letting her go was the most loving gesture he could make. Maybe someday she'd understand that he'd helped her avoid a gigantic mistake.

Exhaustion claimed them both and they slept until the

alarm woke them at four. He threw on his clothes as fast as he could, but she still had to wait for him. She stood there quietly, obviously half asleep. Arms around each other, they made their way back to the house. They pulled off their boots before slipping inside and he walked her to her room.

"You'd better not come in," she murmured.

So true. The chilly morning air had swept away his grogginess and he'd become very aware that he had a half-naked Geena beside him. "I won't." Silently lowering his boots to the floor, he pushed back his hat and cupped her face in both hands. "Thank you." Before she could say anything, he kissed her gently, angling his head so he didn't bump her glasses. He kept his passion in check as he released her.

A night-light shining in the hall bathroom revealed that he'd fogged her lenses, anyway, probably for the last time. He wanted nothing more than to follow her into that room and confess the love that made him ache in ways he'd never thought he could ache. Instead, he picked up his boots and walked away.

At his door, he glanced back to discover that she hadn't moved. She stood exactly as he'd left her and he memorized how she looked in her Captain America sleep shirt because he'd never see her wearing it again. Slowly she raised her hand in farewell. He touched the brim of his hat. Then she turned, walked into her room and closed the door.

He knew then that she'd accepted his decision that they should end it. And why wouldn't she? *Thank you* wasn't exactly a declaration of undying love. More like good manners, and he certainly had those in spades. Her trip to the barn had been her Hail Mary pass, a final attempt to break him down.

No doubt she thought she'd failed, but she'd succeeded beyond her wildest dreams. He loved her with every ounce of his being. And she would never know.

More than once during the shooting of the video that morning, Geena mentally thanked her mother for teaching her the value of discipline and self-reliance. Inheriting some of her mother's stubbornness hadn't hurt anything, either. Although she'd notified everyone except Matt that she planned to leave the ranch after the video was uploaded, she wouldn't get on a plane yet. Not until she knew he was okay.

Fortunately Drew Martinelli was a crackerjack videographer. During the filming Geena learned that the slim brunette had been a hockey star in high school because she could anticipate where the puck would be. That skill gave her a unique advantage as a videographer because she was always ahead of the action instead of following it.

Her dynamic images should accomplish exactly what Geena had hoped for, great PR for Matt and more visibility for Thunder Mountain Academy. Before the afternoon was over, Lexi and Cade had hired Drew to film their wedding. Damon and Phil had debated whether to get a professional video of Sophie at the crawling stage or wait until she was walking. They'd ended up choosing to do both and Rosie had immediately put in an order for copies.

Drew did her edits in Rosie and Herb's office to make sure the final cut met with everyone's approval. That created a standing-room-only situation by the time she'd finished and uploaded the video to the internet.

Later that night, Rosie had champagne and glasses ready for a celebratory toast. As the good cheer flowed around her, Geena soaked it up and reminded herself that, when it came to Matt, it wasn't over until it was over. Scanning the crowded room, she discovered he was working his way toward her.

When he finally made it, she touched her flute to his. "Good job." Taking a sip from her glass, she dared to look him straight in the eye for the first time since they'd started this long day. The depth of emotion she found there took her breath away. That was love, damn it, even if he'd never said so.

He continued to hold her gaze as he took a quick swallow and lowered his glass. "I couldn't have done it without you."

She managed a smile. "True."

"And it was generous of you to offer to be here if my mother shows up. Instead of being appreciative I was rude. I'm sorry."

"Apology accepted."

"But the thing is…" He paused. "I really do need to handle it by myself."

"Which is why my overnight bag is packed and ready to go."

"Does Rosie know you're about to leave?"

"Everybody does." Rosie had insisted she keep the outfit she was wearing and the boots. She'd been offered a place to stay tonight at both Damon and Phil's house and Molly and Ben's. She'd been touched but had politely declined and chosen a hotel in Sheridan, instead. She wasn't feeling her usual social self right now.

He gave her a long look. "Are you okay?"

"Yes." She was more okay now that he'd allowed her to see how much he cared. For a man who was used to disguising his true feelings, that was huge. "Are you?"

"I wouldn't say that. If my birth mom's been following my career online, she's probably seen the video by now and will jump on the opportunity." He took another swallow of his champagne. "Waiting to find out is…"

"Hell?"

"Pretty much."

Geena noticed Rosie walking toward them. "The wait might be over. Here comes Rosie and she looks as if she just bit into something nasty."

Matt sucked in a breath and set down his champagne flute. "Hey, Mom."

"Mindy's on the line. You can take the call in the kitchen." Rosie's cheeks were flushed and her eyes glittered with anger. "I was polite because you asked me to be, but it was one of the hardest things I've ever done."

"Thank you." Matt gathered her close. "Love you, Mom."

"Love you, too, son."

When he released her, he looked over at Geena. "You aren't going to leave right this minute, are you?"

"I'll wait until you get back."

"Thanks." Giving the brim of his hat a decisive tug, he left the room.

His foster mom gazed after him. "Inviting that woman here may be exactly what he needs to do, but I don't have to like it."

"You certainly don't."

"When are you flying out?" Rosie glanced up at her. "In all the confusion I can't remember if you told me."

"I didn't because I'm not flying out tomorrow."

"Oh?"

"I'll be staying in town for a couple more days. I won't tell him, but if at some point you think he might want to know…"

"Got it." Rosie sighed. "That boy is crazy about you."

"That's what gives me hope. And I'm crazy about him, which is why I'm not going anywhere just yet."

Approval shone in Rosie's eyes. "I knew I liked you."

"Same here, Rosie. I'll never forget how you—wow, that was quick. He's coming back already." Her heart ached as she watched him cross the room, his back ramrod straight as if preparing himself to face a firing squad.

All light and warmth had left his expression. He'd locked his emotions away, and when he reached them he spoke with a chilling lack of inflection. "She'll be here in the morning."

Matt didn't sleep much that night. He chose the barn again, which wouldn't make sense to anyone but him. Being there sharpened the pain of Geena's absence, but it also brought him comfort because she'd confessed her love while lying with him on this bed of straw. Saying goodbye to her had been really tough.

Wide-eyed, he waited for dawn and considered the various strategies he'd planned for dealing with his mother. So much depended on her behavior when she arrived. When the sky lightened to the color of rich cream, he saddled Navarre, left a note tacked to Navarre's stall and rode over to his ranch. He could have asked her to meet him there instead of polluting Thunder Mountain with her presence, but instinct had warned him not to let her know about this place.

Tying Navarre to the railing again, he walked over to the grassy spot where he and Geena had made love. The grass was wet with dew and the crushed blades had mostly recovered. Even so, he imagined he could see the outline of her beautiful, naked body as she'd welcomed him into her warm embrace.

Her hairpins glinted in the soft light. He gathered them

up and shoved them into his pocket. He'd decide later if returning them would be insensitive. Probably.

Next he climbed the porch steps and unlocked the front door. Two days ago he'd come through this door to the sound of Geena practicing a tap-dance routine in the master bedroom so she could perform for Rosie. Between the Skype call and working on the video, that hadn't happened. She'd never had her riding lesson with Lexi, either.

As he roamed the empty house remembering how they'd discussed the improvements Damon and Phil could help him make, he came to a decision. He would keep this ranch because Geena believed in his ability to make a home here. Maybe someday he'd accomplish that and be the man she thought he was.

His dad and Cade were in the middle of feeding when he came back to Thunder Mountain, so he gave Navarre a quick rubdown before taking him inside for his grain and flake of hay. The ride had soothed him and he was able to return the cheerful greetings sent his way as he pitched in to do his share.

He made a quick call to Ty down in Cheyenne before breakfast. There was a legal issue concerning his mother that he needed clarified before he saw her, and Ty was able to give him a quick answer.

Being with his family helped calm him even more. He ate a little and participated in the breakfast-table conversation. Lexi had brought Ringo down to see him and Ringo had graciously agreed to sit in his lap and keep two strips of bacon from going to waste. A purring cat turned out to be a terrific stress reducer. Nobody mentioned his mother's visit.

But later, after he'd showered and shaved and gone to

wait for her on the porch, Rosie came out, although she didn't sit down.

Immediately he stood. Rosie had taught him never to remain seated when a lady was standing.

She gazed at him, sympathy in her blue eyes and compassion in every line of her plump body. "Do you want to invite her in? I just need to know if we should clear out of the living room."

"Mom, I don't want her here at all, so I'm definitely not inviting her in. At one time I thought about meeting her in town, but a public place didn't seem right. I don't know what she'll be like or what she'll do."

"I know you don't, son. Just remember we're here if you need backup for any reason."

"Thanks, Mom." He gave her a tight hug. "Love you."

"Love you, too." She patted his cheek. "You'll be fine." Then she went back inside.

He didn't feel fine. He wished he'd taken up whittling so he'd have something to do with his hands, although in the shape he was in he'd likely maim himself with the knife.

The sound of a vehicle coming down the ranch road sent his pulse into the red zone. The engine sputtered and coughed as if it might not last long enough to make the journey. Eventually a dented pickup with a faded blue paint job pulled up in front of the ranch house.

Matt got to his feet as the passenger door opened and an overweight woman with dull brown hair slowly climbed down. He didn't recognize her. Maybe his mother was driving the truck and this was a friend.

Then the woman took off her sunglasses and peered at him. "Matty? Is that you?"

His mother's voice. A chill swept over him even though it was a warm day. "Yes, ma'am." He came down the steps toward her but stopped before he was within touching distance and shoved his hands in his pockets.

He'd wondered if he'd have the urge to hug her. Nope. He might as well be meeting a complete stranger. The person he remembered had been proud of her figure and her glossy black hair. She'd been in her midthirties then, so now she'd be around fifty, but she looked much older.

Her face was puffy, which made her eyes seem smaller. They'd been dulled by age and whatever drugs she'd ingested over the years. She'd piled on the makeup, though, which only made her look worse. "*Yes, ma'am,* is it?" Her comment was delivered with an unbecoming sneer. "Who taught you *that*?"

"My mother."

"The hell I did! You were raised to be a tough smart-ass! None of this *yes, ma'am* and *no, ma'am* crap." She looked around, her avid gaze taking in the ranch house and the barn. "Looks like you had it pretty good here, though."

"Yes, ma'am." He felt a twinge of pity. She really was pathetic.

"Oh, cut it out, Matty. I'm not impressed. You and me, we're poor white trash, so don't go putting on airs. You said on the phone that you had something to discuss with me."

"I do."

"You implied that it involves money and I hope it does. I'm between a rock and a hard place and since you have plenty, I figure you can give your poor mother a—"

"It does involve money." Not only was she pathetic, she was greedy. He might have made some self-centered decisions recently, but he'd never been greedy. He'd never expected a handout, either, and yet she obviously felt entitled to one.

"Okay, now we're talkin'."

Had she turned out to be different, he would have adjusted his plan, but after this brief exchange he knew what needed to be done. She'd given him life and he would permanently settle that debt. He was about to buy his freedom. "I'm prepared to give you a lump sum with a condition attached."

She licked her red lips. "How much?"

He named a figure that made her eyes widen. "But, like I said, there's a condition."

She shrugged. "I don't care."

"I never want to hear from you again." As he said it, he felt self-respect flowing back into his body.

"Matty!" Her mouth dropped open. "That's mean."

"No, it's drawing boundaries. It's self-preservation. It's realizing that I don't have to be defined by my past and I certainly don't have to stay in touch with you. That's my condition. Do you accept?"

"Sure." But her little smile said otherwise.

"It's important that you keep your word, because if you do try to contact me, I'll have you arrested for child abuse."

"That's a laugh. You can't—"

"Turns out I can. According to one of my foster brothers, an excellent lawyer by the way, there's no statute of limitations in Wyoming. So stay away from me or end up in jail. Your choice."

"You are a cold person, Matty."

"No, ma'am, I'm not. A cold person would want revenge. A cold person would have lured you here with the hint of giving you money and instead he'd have cops waiting with a warrant."

Her gaze shifted to the front door. "You don't have cops here, do you?"

"No. Give me your address and I'll send you a cashier's check."

"Hang on." She went back to the truck, said something to the driver and returned with a scrap of paper and a pen. She wrote the information down and handed him the paper. "I need to get going. Lenny's tired of waitin' on me."

"Under the circumstances you'd think he'd put up with the inconvenience."

She sidled close, bringing with her a whiff of cigarette smoke. "He won't be getting a dime. Once that check arrives, I'm leaving him. There's better out there than Lenny." She put on her sunglasses. "So long, Matty."

"So long." He couldn't bring himself to call her anything. Not Mom, for sure, but not Mindy, either. She was nothing to him.

For years she'd been a shadowy memory, a person who might have turned out to have some redeeming qualities, things he hadn't remembered. Not really. In a world full of amazing people like his foster family and Geena, why would he waste another second on someone he was only connected to by an accident of birth?

He watched her climb laboriously into the pickup. Then he continued to stand there as the truck wheezed and clattered around the drive and onto the ranch road. He kept listening until he couldn't hear it anymore. *Gone.* He sagged with relief.

On the heels of that emotion came a powerful surge of joy. He wasn't like her at all. Instead, he was a proud member of the Thunder Mountain Brotherhood and the lucky son of Rosie and Herb Padgett. If he hadn't completely messed things up with Geena, he might... no, that was getting ahead of himself. Anyway, because he'd asked her to leave, she'd be on a plane to Denver by now.

* * *

Heart thumping, Geena drove up to the ranch house and climbed out of the rental car. Rosie had sounded like an excited teenager on the phone.

She must have been watching for the car, because she hurried out onto the porch and down the steps. "I sent him to the barn to muck out stalls." She put a hand on her chest and took a quick breath. "He was driving us crazy."

"How?"

"Going on and on about what an idiot he'd been to insist you go back today. We had to agree. But of course he didn't know I'd already called you."

Geena smiled. "You could have told him I didn't leave."

"It's better if you appear and explain it to him. The shock of seeing you when he thinks you're gone might finally convince him that this is true love we're talking about."

Geena's throat tightened. "Yes, it is."

"Have you been online this morning?"

"Of course. I've been fielding requests for interviews from people eager to talk to Matt about Thunder Mountain. All the negative stuff is old news. We did it, Rosie."

"Mostly *you* did it. Now, get on down there before he takes a notion to come back to the house for some reason and ruins the dramatic moment."

"Okay." Geena figured that if Rosie had grown up in Hollywood she'd have become a director.

"I can guarantee you maybe thirty minutes of privacy. Herb's in the office doing paperwork and Cade's staying in his cabin until I give him the all clear. He mentioned calling one of his brothers about the caretaking job at Matt's ranch."

"So, Matt wants to keep it?"

"Honey, he wants it all, you included. After he sent that woman packing he was a changed man. The realization that he's nothing like her was exactly what he needed, but he had to see her to believe it. Now, go on so you can make a grand entrance."

Geena gave her a quick hug. "Thanks, Rosie."

"You're welcome. It's what I do."

Yes, it certainly was, Geena thought as she walked down to the barn wearing the boots Rosie had given her. Her pants and blouse were clothes she'd brought from LA, but at least she was making this trek in Wyoming-worthy boots. On her way she glanced over at the pasture to admire the horses grazing in it.

After such a short time, the ranch felt like home. But Matt's ranch would feel that way, too, once Damon and Phil made some changes and the place had furniture and a couple of horses in the barn. She yearned to be part of creating that ambience.

Matt had never had a place of his own, but then, neither had she. She'd postponed buying anything in the city and maybe this was why. She envisioned a no-maintenance rental in LA with plenty of room for two. When she was ready to kick back and relax, she belonged on a ranch in Wyoming. With Matt.

Rosie had assured her that he felt the same, but that didn't stop the butterflies from swarming in her stomach as she walked inside the cool interior of the barn. The rhythmic sound of straw being shoveled into a wheelbarrow directed her to a stall near the back of the barn.

Although her boot heels clicked on the wooden aisle, he kept shoveling so he probably hadn't heard her. The wheelbarrow nearly blocked the aisle next to the stall where he was working, but she managed to maneuver around it so she could look in.

He'd pulled off his white T-shirt and tossed it over the open stall door. His back and chest glistened with sweat as his impressive muscles flexed with each movement of the shovel. She almost hated to interrupt him.

Almost. She waited for the brief moment of silence between dumping one load into the wheelbarrow and scooping up another. "Matt."

He wheeled toward her and stood there clutching the shovel. "Geena?"

"I didn't leave today."

He swallowed. "Obviously."

"I didn't leave because I love you."

For one long moment he stared at her. Then he chucked the shovel in the straw and closed the distance between them. But when he was about two feet away he came to an abrupt halt. "I'm sweaty."

"I don't care. Hold me, Matt! Kiss me and tell me you love me as much as I love you, because if you don't, then—"

"I do!" He swept her into his arms. "I love you, Geena." He held her gaze. "I didn't think I had the right, but now everything's different in my mind. That woman is out of my head and out of my life. Which leaves room for us."

"I love the sound of that word. *Us.*"

"Good, because you'll be hearing it a lot." He smiled down at her. "You stayed. I told you to leave but you stayed. How great is that?"

"Yeah, well, when you love someone, you stick around."

"I sure hope so, because I want you to stick around forever, pretty lady. I want you to make love to me in the grass and practice tap dancing in our bedroom."

"*Our* bedroom?"

"I thought of it that way from the minute we walked in."

"Me, too." She looked into blue eyes shining with love. "Now fog up my glasses, cowboy."

Epilogue

Zeke Rafferty hadn't counted on tearing a rotator cuff. Disability insurance was a pricey proposition, so he hadn't taken out a policy. The surgery had wiped out his savings and now he had weeks, maybe even months, before he could go back to trick roping.

So when his foster brother Cade Gallagher called with a job offer that he could do with one arm out of commission, he thanked his lucky stars. "I can absolutely take care of Matt's ranch for a few months," he said. "But I have to be honest with you, bro. I plan to go back to roping as soon as my shoulder heals. If he's looking for a permanent caretaker, I can't in all good conscience take the job."

"Here's how I see it, Zeke. When I heard that you were laid up, I—"

"How did you hear about it, anyway? That's a mystery to me."

"You were in Cheyenne when it happened, right?"

"I was."

"And while you were recovering from surgery you went into Rangeland Roasters for a cup of coffee."

"Several times. They have an excellent brew. Okay, I get it. I talked to Whitney. She's real friendly, which is perfect for someone managing a coffee shop. I've been so busy on the rodeo circuit I haven't kept up. Didn't know ol' Ty was married."

"Luckily Whitney mentioned you to Ty, who called Rosie, who gave me your number. When the planets align like that, I figure you should take the job and we'll worry about finding a replacement later. Besides, if you move back for a few months, you can come to my wedding in August. I would have sent you an invitation but I didn't have an address."

"You and Lexi?"

"Me and Lexi."

Zeke smiled at the pride in Cade's voice when he said that. "Congratulations. You two were always meant to be together."

"Fortunately she finally saw that, too. So, can I tell Matt you're on board? That'll be one less thing he has to deal with."

"By all means, tell him I'm on board. And also tell him I always knew that scandal nonsense was bogus. The Thunder Mountain Brotherhood doesn't pull crap like that."

"Indeed we don't. Listen, I just realized I have no authority to offer you a salary, so who knows what Matt will pay you. He's a straight shooter, though, so it'll be a fair wage."

"Don't worry about it. A free place to stay and a little

money for food is all I'll need. I'm obliged, Cade. I didn't know how I'd navigate the next few months."

"Yeah, and that reminds me that we shouldn't have had to find this out by the back door. You should have contacted Rosie and Herb right away when you ran into a spot of trouble."

"I feel like they did enough when we were there." Zeke exhaled. "I'm not the kind of guy who goes running back home to—"

"Hey, we're the brotherhood, remember? We stick together and we look out for our own."

"That's...that's good to hear. Really good. See you soon, bro." Zeke disconnected the call. He'd been a lone wolf all his life, even while he was a foster kid at Thunder Mountain. He'd vowed that once he was capable of living on his own, he'd make sure he never needed anybody.

But the torn rotator cuff had punched a big hole in that plan. For the time being, he'd take the job offered to him and be grateful, even if it chafed that he'd been brought so low that he required help. In the future he'd plan better so that wouldn't happen again.

* * * * *

Want more heroes from the
THUNDER MOUNTAIN BROTHERHOOD?
Watch for the next book in
Vicki Lewis Thompson's miniseries,
SAY YES TO THE COWBOY, coming July 2017,
only from Harlequin Special Edition!